ORDEAL AT
BLOOD RIVER

ORDEAL AT BLOOD RIVER

JAMES WARNER BELLAH

CUTTING EDGE

ISBN-13: 978-1-954840-36-2

Published by
Cutting Edge Books
PO Box 8212
Calabasas, CA 91372
www.cuttingedgebooks.com

CHAPTER ONE

Fɪʀsᴛ Lɪᴇᴜᴛᴇɴᴀɴᴛ Fʟɪɴᴛʀᴇᴅɢᴇ Cᴏʜɪʟʟ, Second Cavalry, detached, was traveling back to civilization with the ghosts and the papers of three dead men—the final, tragic report of the Columbia River Survey. That had been such a savage two-year nightmare of duty that a sense of utter unreality still shadowed the inner chambers of his mind. Aboard the brig *Lucy,* all the way down the Pacific Coast from Portland to San Francisco en route to rejoin his regiment at Fort Starke in the Territory, Cohill had fought himself doggedly back to humanity with the sunlight and the salt air and quiet communion with his very real soldier's God.

Over the river line of his middle thirties, with almost a score of years in the Service, Cohill had only one well-worn silver bar to his cavalry-yellow shoulder strap to show for his life. Very low-ranking still in the tiny, slow-promotion Army, in spite of three wounds and four major frontier campaigns, he was little more than a tactical killer with an acquired instinct for self-preservation. A man tightly bound in his own professional abilities, he had known few women of his own station in life—and only one that he could ask to pay the sacrificial penalties of sharing it. She hadn't.

Off the Farallons, after five days at sea, Cohill was almost his own man again in tranquility of mind. The next morning as the *Lucy* beat up the Bay through the Golden Gate and past Fort Point toward wooded Alcatraz Island, the reveille gun from the Presidio woke him. With his face at the porthole of his cabin, he saw the colors go up the pole over the raw barrack sheds of the post and felt warmth in his heart. There were troops there, Cohill's way of life.

Then the harbor boat came alongside the *Lucy* with mail and papers, and the headlines of last night's San Francisco *Evening Bulletin* struck Cohill like a thonged quirt across the eyes.

DISASTER ON THE GILA RIVER
SECOND CAVALRY DETACHMENT WIPED OUT
FORTS YUMA AND MOJAVE LONG UNREPORTED
Despatches by Central Pacific telegraph relayed east from Tucson by way of Fort Leavenworth, Kansas, advise us that a force of the Second United States Cavalry was annihilated two weeks ago in a desert action in the Arizona country of the western New Mexico Territory. No indication of the number of casualties has as yet been received. When the Apaches began to sack the rim settlements of the Arizona country east of the Colorado River last September, the Second Cavalry concentrated at Tucson. It is assumed that the disastrous action took place as the result of an effort to establish contact across the desert between Tucson and the Department of California garrisons on the Colorado at Fort Yuma and Fort Mojave. The Presidio admits that routine couriers from both those outposts are overdue.

As he read it, Cohill felt as if personal injury had been done him. Whoever those dead men in their dirty blue shirts were, he would know most of them. Flint Cohill had invested so much of his living in the Second Cavalry that the regiment was like an old and honored wife for whom a deep affection endures on the solid basis of the remembered ecstasies of youth.

When the brig anchored he said goodbye to Hans Bendrodt, the *Lucy's* fat Danish master, to whiskey-soaked

Calvinist MacIlvary, her steward and supercargo, and climbed down the side-ladder to her longboat in the golden morning sun of San Francisco Bay. He was in uniform, with gloves and saber belt. He drew his elk-cased saber from the straps of his horsehide field trunk and stuck it like a walking stick, under his left arm—he would hook it in later to report to the Presidio under arms.

As the *Lucy's* four men pulled the longboat toward the end of Meiggs Wharf, Cohill stared across toward the shanty settlement of San Francisco, dice-thrown sketchily across the Bay side of the hills. The waterfront was still hulk-scabrous from the days of the gold rush, the whole foreshore built out with rotting, gutted ships, where the gold-mad crews had deserted them.

Tied up alongside Meiggs Wharf were four square-rigged ships, two on each side below the T-cross of the pierhead. Down the center of the pier there was a disordered, high-stacked ridge-line of broken cargo with men and boom whips working it.

Even at this offshore distance and low to the water in the longboat, Cohill saw that the cargo working party on the dock was mixed military and civilian—and that there was trouble. A man with a red neckrag leaped up the cargo dump and swung a roundhouse punch to flatten a soldier in blue, and booted down on him to clobber his prone body.

Then suddenly above the mill of angry men on the dock, there was a horse in belly-slings frantically kicking against the beautiful California sky. Evidently the animal, a deep-chested, small-headed Arab, screaming in panic at his sudden footloose flight from security, had come up on tackle from the hold of the nearest ship. His thrashing legs half spun him in the hoisting gear that held him high. The faces of the scrabbling men below flashed upward in sudden fear, and legs moved rapidly to spread out fast from the area. As the boom swung the stallion out overhead, the *Lucy's* longboat touched hard on the hemp fenders of the dock ladder below.

For a moment, climbing the ladder, Flint Cohill could see nothing on the dock above. Then he was head and shoulders up, clinging to the ladder in stupefied amazement. With the Arab's flailing hooves not six feet above the dock planking, thrashing still in the narrow space between the cargo dump and the ship's side, the stallion suddenly doubled up and quivered, tense to the sound of a woman's voice, *"Turk!"*

Her slim figure was below the suspended animal and slightly to one side, one of her arms raised in rigid signal to the winch man on the ship, her fist clenched; white bloused, her short yellow hair clubbed with a narrow ribbon and, amazingly, waist to ankles, the long black silk tights of a circus acrobat. Her slender legs were slightly bent at the knees in tension. Then the fingers of her upraised hand opened and starfished. Slowly the sling lowered away and at the exact moment the great stallion's hooves touched down, the young woman cat-sprang to his back, her knees vising into him, her hands tearing the sling releases free.

Cohill stood frozen at the sight. For the break of a second, the huge stallion trembled mightily, his legs stiffly thrust in the tangle of slings and guide lines. Then he gathered like a coiled spring and came streaking for the open broadway where Cohill stood, pirouetting high above the scrambling men, hatcheting at them with his forehooves.

Cohill leaped out of the way onto the pile of stores, landed high and standing and half whipped around as the Arab tore past him. The girl was riding the beast in wild exultation, her hands twisted into his wind-torn mane, her lips drawn back over white teeth. As she thundered by, Flint heard the soft keen of her voice— half in ecstasy, half goading the Arab to his full head for the ultimate exhaustion she must force him to, to bring him down.

In the open space of dock head, the stallion circled close— spun on his own shadow—and came tearing back past Cohill again.

Setting aside for a moment the insanity of a woman up on a stallion at all, Cohill's eyes were riveted on the rider. He had never seen a man nor a Pawnee more a part of a mount. No bridle, no saddle, no girth—nothing but the will to control. Down the dock to the shore and in a long roll of staccato hooves, and out across the open flat at the base of the hill-strewn town.

Cohill was halfway up the heap of broken cargo, where his spring had landed him. He reached with a gloved hand to the cluttered pile to lever himself down to the dock planking again; over blanket bales dusted white from stave-burst flour barrels, uncrated McClellan saddles and sacked coffee mounded in with ordnance cases of Sharps carbines, the coffee broken to an ankle-deep cascade of pungent black beans. A whip of anger lashed Cohill's mind at the wastage as he climbed down over it, for he had known hungry soldiers in his time—had been on the grisly end of ammunition short supply, and had hated waste ever since.

The rioting crowd of men thrown back under the stallion's threat was clotting in again, shouting in deep-throated anger. A civilian workman grabbed the leg of the blue-uniformed man who was down in the cargo pile, spun him by it from the pile to the planking. The soldier's head struck an iron bollard, and cracked like a kicked wooden box. From the top of the pile a case of carbines crashed down, splintering open on the stringpiece, spilling half the pieces overside into the water.

Cohill leaped fast onto the pile of stores again, his angry eyes searching the mob for gang bosses or non-coms. He scrambled toward the core of the fight, looking sharp for a break in it to pressure it apart from a point of control. He saw the point suddenly where four men were down and sprang upright into the open space, shouting to a soldier *"You men there—break it off!"* then gave them his back as he turned sharp to face the civilian stevedores. "Move out of this!" and he started toward them. "This is United States Government property!"

There was sudden silence over the eye of the riot. Men fell away and gaped at him. Cohill walked toward the group of civilian workmen, making his pace deliberate. The provost marshal's guard couldn't have levered the fight apart quicker. Still facing the civilians, Cohill called back over his shoulder to the men, "Fall in the fatigue detail—guiding right—*on this ship's gangplank!*" and he whipped his cased saber like a stick to indicate. He heard men shuffle behind him to obey the order.

Then he stepped across to the inert form lying beside the iron bollard and to his horror he saw the shoulder straps of a second lieutenant of cavalry—saw death gauntly masking the youngster's well-boned face. He knelt uselessly to feel the heart, and fury tore him. He stood up, his face savage. "Damn your eyes! You've killed an Army officer!" He walked slowly back toward them. "Who's in charge of you!" Their eyes glanced quickly to a man still down on the planking in the thick snow from a ruptured flour barrel. Cohill yanked the man to his feet. He was a burly Levantine in torn white undershirt and coverall pants, growling in animal rage as he clawed the sweat-pasted flour that fouled his eyes. He had startling yellow eyes—bright yellow, fired lighter than burnished gold.

"Well damn *me!*" he said fervently to Cohill's close face, and he shook his tight dark curls to one side. In each of his ear lobes there was a tiny golden earring.

"*Give me your name!*" Cohill's harsh voice pressed him.

The man inhaled deeply. Then his eyes swept contemptuously from Cohill's in a side cut and he looked at the slovenly formed line of the fatigue party. It was about company strength—forty to fifty—drawn up in two ranks now, guided on the foot of the nearest gangplank. Yellow Eyes spat in contained fury and shouted at the detail, "Before you rupture yourselves—*stan' at ease!*" and the line broke from awkward attention at once. Then he turned his leonine head sharply the other way and thrust a massive hand to the nearest civilian—shoved in short fury so that the man staggered heavily, "Git your hundred-a-month tourists back aboard the *Clan Cameron,* Boldoni!"

Temper burst like a flawed gun breech in Cohill. *"When I give an order to troops—nobody amends it or interferes with it!"*

"Well!" Yellow Eyes exhaled loudly on the word. Then he swept his right arm straight and fast to thrust Cohill slightly from balance and stalked through him. At the base of the cargo pile, he stooped to a flung coat and snatched it up, shrugged his knotted shoulders into it and turned back to Cohill. His shoulders were tabbed with a major's greenish gold-threaded leaves. He buttoned the blouse slowly, his eyes hard on Cohill. He lifted one coveralled leg and dusted at the clinging flour—still watching Cohill. Lifted the other leg. Dusted. From the side pocket of his uniform blouse, he drew a battered officer's kepi, slapped it to his thigh once, then settled it to his oily curls, with both hands sweeping the hair clear at the sides, so that the sun splintered on the tiny rings in his ears.

"Now, what's *your* name, mister?"

The fiber of a regular is the innate ability to dismiss all personality from the fact of rank, but the fury in Cohill still held him. "That is a dead officer there, sir." He pointed an outraged finger. "My name is Cohill. Second Cavalry."

The major looked over at the body. He said, "I warned the schoolboy not to mix up with these roustabouts. Sergeant St. Yves!" he shouted, "Blanket Mister Haight's body and have it littered up to the Presidio." Then he stared at Cohill, one eyebrow up. "Carracoe, me—" the major told him, and with a gesture to indicate the dock and ships, "—commanding. Unless you're reporting to me —get t'hell on about your business, for I can't stomach an officer who wears gloves!"

With slow deliberation, Cohill stripped his left glove. Then his right. Major Carracoe's mouth opened as if he had been tapped in the pit of the stomach. There was quick disbelief in his eyes, then the vibrant dominance went out of them under abject fear.

Cohill's hands had no fingernails, only scaling, half-healed skin where the nails had been. The flesh of his hands to his wrists was leprous gray, the epidermis skeined and sloughing under a coating of yellow goose grease.

"Put on your gloves!" Carracoe's intensity of voice half choked him. He doubled his own great hands into half-up fists, then his fingers relaxed, and his hands cupped open, palms upward, almost to implore Cohill. "Get out of here, mister. Off this dock—and out of my sight!" The major crinkled his eyes shut and made a thumb and forefinger gesture across his strong white teeth that had the implication of ritual. Then he turned and pushed blindly through the fatigue party, and up the *Clan Cameron's* gangplank. He was a big man, but he seemed to scuttle.

Cohill drew on his loose gloves again, carefully, to cover his mutilated hands. One of the *Lucy's* men had come up behind him from dock head with his horsehide field trunk shouldered. The sailor winked. "Haunt layin' sign 'e made. You evil marked him, sir. Yellow-eyed Gypsy. Weird blokes. See sperrits they do."

At dock end Cohill raised his cased saber, flicked it to signal a carryall across the dock flats. "Apaches burn your hands, mister?" Cohill gave the sailor two bits for loading the field trunk on. "Frozen," Cohill said. "Not burned. But they're half-mended now."

As the carryall headed across toward the winding shore road up to the Presidio, Cohill looked back and saw the two litter-bearers turn off the dock, carrying young Haight's blanketed body. As they put it down to spit on their hands, the dead boy's booted feet moved slightly with the jolt and Cohill looked away. He thanked his stars that in the course of his own duties he would have no further contact with Major Carracoe or the criminally wasteful disorder of Meiggs Wharf.

CHAPTER TWO

AS THE CARRYALL MOVED SLOWLY along the shorefront road around the rise of Telegraph Hill, Flint Cohill saw the Arab stallion off to his right with the yellow-haired girl walking ahead. She had apparently turned the animal into the foreshore to run him out on packed sand, and she was leading him back now to intercept the road. Leading him by voice alone—to cool out.

With a flat open space on either side of the shore trail, she spoke him into circling. Spoke him from a walk to a trot. Widened his circle slightly and by voice again, brought him up to an easy, circling gallop. Then she sprinted behind him as he passed her, raced across the circle, leaped easily and landed standing on his back. Landed half crouched at the knees, then stood slimly erect with incredible ease and grace. Almost at once she was on the ground again in the center of the circle, watching the Arab intently. By voice she reversed his circling movement to counterclockwise and leaped to his back again. From standing, she then doubled her body, placed her hands on the animal's rump and, arching her spine easily, thrust her slender legs upward, flashing black silk in the sun, and completed a full circle riding his gallop on her hands.

Then she back-flipped to her feet and came off in a forward somersault to her feet again, on the ground. As she landed she saw the stopped carryall in the roadway.

Across three hundred yards, Cohill felt her indignation. His tight lips sliced to a smile of admiration, he raised his kepi slightly above his head and bowed in appreciation of the performance, replacing the kepi. With just the faintest head toss of defiance, she spoke the Arab out of his circling—brought him to her. Stepped to his head as he whinnied and arched his neck, touched his cheek with the flat of her hand, and then, with no visible effort, leaped again easily to mount conventionally and walked him to the road, leaning to him straight-backed, talking to him. One hand to his withers, the other smoothing her wind-tangled hair, she said, "That was not done for your benefit, sir. I thought Turk and I were alone."

"I'm sure you did," Cohill told her. "No other thought was in my mind. Beyond and above your Cossack riding, you handle him magnificently!"

"Nonsense," she said abruptly, still caught in her annoyance.

"On a narrow freight-cluttered dock it is not nonsense." Cohill shook his head. "Not with a riot all about him. Not after a horse has been penned up in a ship's hold—for how long?"

"Since Mazatlán," she said. "I've just made arrangements to stable and exercise him at the Presidio—on a courtesy charity basis until we sail again."

"I beg your pardon?"

"For what?" she asked him, and he had a stilted feeling that she was purposely prodding the deep embarrassment that she must know he felt at her proximity in those black silk tights.

"The Presidio is an Army post," he said.

"Quite so," she nodded, "whereas Turk and I were lately with Willebrandt's International Circus." Her eyes danced with inner laughter. "Horse and woman—of quite a different color—than Army. The circus became stranded for debt in Mazatlán. Senator Bentinck's kindness had us released from the Mexican authorities when the *Clan Cameron* put into Mazatlán on its way north here from Panama." She put a hand to the Arab's neck and her inner laughter deepened at the slow reaction in his eyes. "We are quite shabby people, Turk and I."

"Oh come," he said, "you are deliberately chivvying me with this talk. Who is Senator Bentinck?"

"He heads the Colorado River Expedition. The four ships at Meigg's Wharf are chartered to him. The *Isthmian Queen* and the *Thomas Hastings* arrived here a week ahead of us. We are transshipping supplies from them. Only the *Clan Cameron* and the *Amos Orr* are to go to the Colorado. We carry a company of militia soldiers—as well as a hundred colonists."

Six or seven years younger than Cohill—twenty-seven or twenty-eight at the outside—her face held great dignity when the laughter faded from her eyes, but with a veiled feminine maturity beyond her years that may have been the result of her circus way of life. He judged by her accent that she was from the East.

Cohill was a wordless man, stilted in his manners by years of the frontier, half-animal in his deeper instincts, with no very deft hand for women ever. Her open, easy manner only increased his own unease.

"You have apparently traveled widely," he said, and because his words sounded horribly stiff, he was impelled to get out of the carryall now, touch his kepi in formality, and give her his name. Her eyes watched him for a moment, searching him out curiously as he stood there below her. Then she nodded slightly in acknowledgment of his name and said, "Athena."

For an embarrassed moment, Cohill was under the impression that she had said some word or phrase in a foreign tongue, something about him for her own amusement alone, for there was the inner laughter in her eyes once more. Cohill heated slightly at the cheekbones when it came to him that Athena must be her first name.

"No last name?" he asked.

"Quite a complicated one," she said, "but if you wish it, you may have it." The smile faded abruptly from her eyes. "I am the Countess Athena von und zu Hortsendorff-Saxe-Schweringen," she said deliberately, and with a slight twist of her body as she sat her horse above him, she held her hand down toward him.

"Come," Cohill chuckled. "A circus billing? That name? Whatever it was you said it was?"

She drew her underlip briefly between her teeth and her eyes widened slightly. "You can be a very insolent man," she told him, "but you will still acknowledge my hand."

He raised his own hand to hers then and she placed her fingers upon his glove. He bowed slightly, watching her eyes. "*Not* a circus billing," she said coldly. "My husband was Rittmeister, the Count Paul of Hortsendorff-Saxe-Schweringen, the King of Württemberg's Own Household Hussars." She pronounced it *Hutzars*. "Aide-de-camp to His Majesty."

"I was extremely rude, it seems then," Cohill said in apology. "For which I am sorry."

"Don't be," she tossed her head in a gesture of derision. "The Count was compelled to resign his commission for marrying a circus rider. I was quite beneath the necessary social requirements for a Household Officer's wife, I assure you. And not nearly fat enough."

There are few things more irritating than a rejected apology. At any rate, Cohill was sufficiently piqued to overcome his customary stiffness. "You seem to deride yourself. A moment ago, you were extremely proud. Why do you do that? First, the one false pose, then the other?"

It put her at no loss. She answered him at once. "Because in spite of my present clothing of performer's tights, you got out into the road to pay me a gentleman's courtesy," she said evenly. "So I gave you a Countess in return," she smiled. "That was the least I could do. Then you threw me away for a mountebank. So I admitted that I was—to embarrass you for my own embarrassment. Are we even?"

Cohill frowned. "I have no skill at small talk—but if I may attempt a compliment," and his frown twisted into a slight smile, "I might say that the Count—is a most fortunate man."

"You would be very wrong then," she said solemnly, "for he was a most unfortunate man. He sold his sword to Inigo Barras. The Count was executed by firing squad in Guadalajara two years ago." Then an expression shadowed her eyes that she did not wish him to see, for she turned quickly from him. "Good day to you, sir," and with slight pressure of her left knee she turned the Arab's head, stretching him in full gallop at once up the road in the direction of the Presidio, leaving Cohill standing in a maelstrom of corded dust with a feeling of awkwardness and insufficiency that he resented deeply.

Under the ramada of headquarters at the Presidio, Cohill stripped the elkskin case from his scabbarded saber, hooked the weapon in to report—knocked and opened the door marked "Adjutant." The office was empty—but only for a moment. Then an inner door opened abruptly on a shrieking hinge and an iron-gray colonel of cavalry with a fistful of papers stepped out. He stopped short in utter disbelief. "Cohill, God bless my soul!"

MacClendon Alshard, the old First Squadron Commander in Cohill's early days with the Second—later to command the regiment at a bare forty years of age. Cohill said "*Colonel* Alshard!" and deep pleasure livened his solemn face.

Alshard dropped the papers, slapped them down hard on his adjutant's desk. "Where in *hell* have you dropped from, Cohill?" and he half circled about Flint as if to turn him with his hands, looking him over like a horse he was going to buy. "But the whole survey party was reported to have been murdered along the Columbia's headwaters!"

"I got out alive," Cohill said, "with one Modoc guide. I have the personal papers of the three other officers—and the consolidated reports that come to nothing but failure and disaster, unfortunately, sir."

Colonel Alshard nodded. "You've come to the right place. We specialize in bad news here."

"I saw last night's newspaper. Have you the Second Cavalry casualty lists yet, sir?"

"No," Alshard said. "I have only the barest word so far — the same as the newspapers have carried. No official notification. Come in, Cohill," and he indicated the door to his inner office, pulling it to after them as they went through. He placed a chair for Cohill, dropped heavily into one himself, offered cigars, flagged out the match, and sat for a moment in the blue haze of tobacco smoke. "I suppose you are in transit to report back to the Second?"

"That is how my orders read, sir. From the agent officer in Portland—endorsed to the Commanding Officer, the Presidio of San Francisco—for transportation east to Fort Starke."

Colonel Alshard leaned back in his chair, stretching his booted legs straight out before him. "I wish I had never left the regiment," he said devoutly. "That was straight-line living—when the civilians' war of '61-'65 ended," he smiled, "and the frontier fighting had to begin again after a four-year hiatus. Ah well, the job goes on—and becomes more complicated. But at least we try to make a country with the scant tools they give us." He drew in his legs, stood up and crossed to the wall map of the Department of California and the empty reaches of the raw New Mexico Territory beyond the Rio Colorado. "The trouble began out here when they made California a state—isolated from the rest of the states by this vast empty stretch of territory between."

To the east of the great spine of the California mountains, he ran his finger down the north-south trace of the Colorado River through the Arizona country from the Grand Cañon to its mouth in Mexican territory. "From out here on the coast, the river is our only feasible port of entry to the western territory that we are now beginning to call Arizona. We use the Mexican mouth of the river to come in by, under our Treaty of Guadalupe Hidalgo—with Mexico." Alshard smiled faintly. "The men call it 'Blood River,' but if the historians were fair, Cohill, they would rename the Colorado 'Lieutenants' River.' Lieutenant Couts first went through to Yuma right after the Mexican War and on out to San Diego on the coast south of here. Lieutenant Whipple explored the river in 1854—for a railway route along the 35th Parallel. In 1857 and '58, Lieutenant Joseph Yves navigated four hundred and twenty-five miles of its length in a portable steamboat shipped in pieces from Philadelphia. Lieutenant Tipton commanded his escort. Two of my Lieutenants command the two small garrisons at Fort Yuma and Fort Mojave now," he frowned slightly. "If we still have those two garrisons."

He put a finger on Fort Yuma, about seventy bird-flown miles north of the Colorado's delta on the Gulf. Then he put his finger on Fort Mojave, a good two hundred and fifty river miles upstream of Fort Yuma. "We supply and relieve these two posts by ship out of San Francisco—sailing around Baja and up the Gulf and transshipping to river steamers. A long sea-haul, but the troops are at least not desert-beaten on arrival."

Cohill eyed the distance scale and then the map to time and space the Butterfield Overland Mail Route south through Reina de Los Angeles and San Diego where the old Gila Trail forks east to Fort Yuma—six hundred miles from San Francisco, with the lower Mojave, the Anza and the Barrego sands lying bleached and oven-baked across a good third of the way overland to the Colorado.

"Standing orders," the colonel nodded to the map, "call for a monthly courier overland to me from both Mojave and Yuma. It is confidential to you that as of today both couriers are sixty-seven days overdue and last month's trace couriers are unreported. Telegraph has been almost continually out since the Apache became active again." He was not complaining—there was no faint note of frustration in his voice, but when he finished speaking, the silence seemed to thicken almost visibly in the smoke-filled air of the tiny office. Nor did Cohill consider answering the colonel. To them both this was an old story, a story of too few men, too far apart. Both men returned to their chairs to sit down heavily.

"This expedition—" Cohill looked in tentative question at the Colonel, "the one loading at Meigg's Wharf, sir?"

Colonel Alshard's face clenched in sudden dark anger and he made a visible effort at control, wiping his hand heavily across his nose and mouth. "It's not an expedition in any sense I ever heard of. It's an undisciplined rabble armed and fed by government surplus. This Rutherford Bentinck is an ex-United States senator. Former member of the Army Committee. Appointive Governor now to Western New Mexico Territory—whatever that may turn out to be when he gets there." It was obvious to Cohill that Colonel Alshard was choosing his words carefully against an impulse to be bitterly critical. "What earthly political cabal induced Congress to authorize this colonizing expedition in threatening times like these is more than I know. Furthermore Bentinck operates under exempted orders; under direct authority from Washington, that is. Which means that I cannot touch him. As Department Commander, I cannot prevent his expedition's going into the Colorado country: my garrison lieutenants cannot control him after he gets there; and I am constrained by covering orders to cooperate to the fullest if Bentinck requests me to. Outside of that—I cannot touch him." Alshard opened both his hands across his knees to relieve his tension, then he clenched them into fists and buffeted his knees sharply once. "I need not tell you, Cohill, what an intolerable position this is for a commander to find himself in. Having an agency scot-free to operate within his command—an agency over which he has no control!"

Watching the colonel, Cohill felt the older man's righteous indignation as if it were an odor in the nostrils.

"I have, however," Alshard said, "put the relief detachment for the Colorado River garrisons aboard his ships—to his deep resentment. But the law allows me the right of commandeer for troop passage aboard any ship leaving for the Colorado—so I took that right. It was all I had."

It was instinctive in Cohill to realize that Colonel Alshard as an Army officer had gone as far in his critical attitude as he was going to go. But instinctively also he knew that there was more to it. Then, surprisingly, Alshard said, "But that is not all of the story. The rest is educated guesswork with no fact to rest a premise on. Nevertheless it is there like an ominous shadow over all of it. Does the name of Inigo Barras mean anything to you? Sometimes called 'General' Barras?"

Cohill moved a leg slightly. The name did mean something and yet again it didn't. Then suddenly it did. *He sold his sword to Inigo Barras. My husband was executed by firing squad in Guadalajara two years ago.*

There was a perfunctory rap upon the office door, which immediately opened to admit the post contract surgeon, Doctor de Canova, a bent-shouldered, gangling figure with extremely thick lenses to his spectacles. "I'm preparing Lieutenant Haight's body for burial—"

"Doing *what?*" Alshard flung himself full around. "Haight's *dead?*"

"As dead as he'll ever be, Colonel. I think you should see the body."

Alshard reached for his kepi. "Come along," he said to Cohill.

The post hospital was a two-room picket-board structure set up diagonally across from quartermaster stores, the front room a ward with four men in the beds. They went through to the back. Lieutenant Haight's body was sheeted on the wooden operating table, his boots and uniform piled on the floor beside. De Canova moved to the head. "The skull," he said, "is depressed with a basal fracture—but that did not cause death. This stab wound did."

De Canova folded the sheet down to disclose the upper abdomen. There was a dried smear of blood under the lower rib on the left side, and as the doctor touched the stiffening flesh between thumb and forefinger, the lips of a tiny wound opened. "I went in." The doctor reached to an instrument tray and held up a crusted Aldous probe. "The wound is about seven inches deep. It pierced the lung diagonally and struck into a heart ventricle."

"Never mind the medical jargon. Say it, De Canova."

"Stiletto, I believe, sir. Stabbed in, by an upthrust."

"You're saying murder?"

The doctor shrugged. "That is a legal expression—not medical."

Back in his own office again, Colonel Alshard closed his door and paced back and forth slowly in apparent agitation; then he sat down and faced Cohill, evidently come to decision.

"Cohill," he said, "I am not putting you into a dead man's boots. From the moment you walked in on me—you were the man—not Haight. But Haight was the only available officer I had until you reported. Young and inexperienced—but the others are too old and inactive. Had Haight lived, it would still be you."

Cohill raised his head sharply and stared for a moment at the colonel. He felt a cold, defensive reaction, which he put down at once, for never in his service had he asked for an assignment for personal reasons—nor begged off one.

"You will take command of Haight's detachment on the *Clan Cameron*," Alshard said, "with orders to relieve the Colorado River garrisons at Fort Yuma and Fort Mojave. My adjutant will give you all the administrative details —and endorse your present orders for this temporary duty en route to rejoin your regiment."

In the brief moment that he sat immobile before acknowledging the order, Cohill had the quick animal reaction of feeling trapped. It was not personal, even though he had every right to expect, after the last two years, routine travel orders to return to regimental duty. It was mechanical and instinctive and held no logic that he could argue in his mind. Then quite shockingly it came to him that Alshard was a man who was also trapped in a very tangible fashion. A fettered man, constrained to the responsibilities of his higher rank with no adequate facilities to discharge them. Meeting his obligations with the incisive mind that had raised him to eagles well on the sunny side of fifty, but detesting the limitations that prevented him from doing the job in the thorough fashion with which he felt it should be done.

Cohill stood up. Knuckles on the closed door caught his "Yes, sir," before he could say it, and the door opened to a stoutish civilian well into the sixties, firmly belted under a dropped stomach, his hand held out to the colonel in greeting, his painfully mottled face wrinkled in a jovial grin.

Alshard said, "Good morning, marshal" and they shook hands. "This is Lieutenant Cohill. Mr. Eudaley is the United States marshal in San Francisco, Cohill."

"How do," Eudaley said, and stood quite patiently waiting for Cohill to leave, studying him with mild question in his old eyes. "Young Haight," Alshard said quietly, "was done to death on Meigg's Wharf earlier this morning. Mister Cohill is taking over his command."

Eudaley squinched his lips together and whistled air softly. He turned his head then and gave Cohill an appraising glance. Alshard and the marshal sat for a moment watching each other's eyes, each in silent consideration of things that had obviously been discussed before between them. Cohill watched them narrowly, for whatever this situation was, it had now become a part of his professional life. After a moment the marshal struck both flat hands softly to the tops of his thighs.

"I won't say Inigo Barras isn't in San Francisco," he said heavily, "but if he is, I can't find him. I ran down both my informers' stories—and mark you they both want to kill Barras for running out on them at Guadalajara, so if they could find him for me or themselves they would. They can't, for all they have is rumor. How much have you told Cohill?"

"I had just started."

"I know how you started, too," Marshal Eudaley smiled. "Army fashion. I'll tell it police fashion. Mister—" he tapped Cohill's knee "—you've bought yourself a hell of a job. This Bentinck is no good. Official as all hell and operating out here with government authority—but no damned good—to himself, to his friends or to the United States."

Cohill watched the older man. "It reads like this in the record," Eudaley said. "Two years ago this Rutherford Bentinck was sent by the Senate down to Mexico as chairman of the United States Neutrality Commission. Down there, he met Inigo Barras, the filibuster. Some say he saved him from execution. After that Bentinck got suddenly rich. Overnight. Sailor rich. He spent money in Washington like just off a ship and it's my bet that the money was Inigo Barras' Mexican loot, and that it helped lobby up this expedition—for more loot. Barras is worse than no good. He's a cutthroat, screaming that God justifies him in all his acts. God-crazy and man-brutal. Now come to the present facts. Bentinck with this expedition arrives here in force you might say, and there is a strong rumor that Barras is here in San Francisco too; but it ain't rumor that what's left of Inigo Barras' Legion of Liberation—under their damned blue Southern Cross flag —is still robbing and pillaging in northern Sonora and that the senator's goin' down there into the Colorado country with a hundred roustabout colonists scraped up from gutters in the East, surplus supplies for a small army, and a territorial no-good recruit militia company commanded by an ear-ringed Gypsy drunk."

Cohill sat quietly waiting for the marshal to go on. The marshal said, "Colonel Mac here can't stop it—because Washington has tied his hands. But mebbe I can. Give me the full word on young Haight's death and mebbe I can hold a murderer—with the rest of the expedition as accessories. Least I'll try."

It had been in Cohill's mind since it happened. Lying in loose pieces, until Dr. de Canova had pinched his fingers to that tiny wound in Haight's upper abdomen. It didn't quite come together then, but it damned well did now. "That militia fatigue detail was in stable coveralls and undershirts," he said. "Haight was in his blue uniform blouse. The only one in blue. I saw him struck down first, on top of the cargo pile. A civilian workman struck him and went down on top of him, using his boots. Man had a red sweatrag around his neck. Line up the civilians and pick out the red neckrags. Search those men for thin knives with stiletto blades. The man who has one——"

CHAPTER THREE

RUDOLPH SNAVELY, THE ADJUTANT, was a sixty-three year old silver-buttoned storekeeper captain with the channels of his mind cut inexorably in routine, frozen to the Army system like wheel ruts in the winter Dakota country. Patiently Cohill listened to the captain's long-winded explanations, while his mind grasped the whole situation and began filing and sorting probabilities.

By rotation, the relief platoon for the Colorado was the second platoon of the Presidio's own garrison troop, already detached under Lieutenant Haight and at present building stalls for their mounts in the 'tween decks aboard the *Clan Cameron*. The other regular cavalry troop, which, together with the Presidio's garrison troop, constituted the entire California Department cavalry, was already in one platoon garrison at Fort Yuma and one platoon garrison at Fort Mojave.

The operating procedure was that Yuma was relieved by the fresh troops. The Yuma garrison then moved upstream and relieved Mojave. The Mojave garrison went back downriver and out by ocean ship to San Francisco. Simple enough on paper but the actual fact was that because of low appropriations and remoteness from a practical concept of the problem by Washington, the whole thing was a tacit admission that there was one trained, professional soldier to about every four thousand square miles of territory that the Army was required to control.

Captain Snavely had the supply and equipment tables reduced to an exact formula for this routine yearly relief. He was a man who could not vary a single item by a hair. All you had to do was take copies of what he had laboriously drawn up, fit them into what was practical from a troop standpoint, and make a personal reconnaissance for the usual method of swapping overs and glomming shorts.

With the administrative picture well in his mind by one o'clock, Cohill was getting ready to take off for Meigg's Wharf when Colonel Alshard sent for him. "Two things, Cohill. Marshal Eudaley is certain of it, and I cannot overlook the fact that Haight's killing may have been deliberate: an effort to deprive the relief detachment of its only officer. Therefore I want you to carry a pocket gun here in San Francisco."

"Very well, sir," Cohill hesitated—it was not in him to make excuses—but he went on, "I expect de Canova can fix up my hands. They had a bad bout with freezing and it will probably be some days before I can use a hand gun."

Colonel Alshard eyed him. "Be sure you know what you're doing, Cohill. This is no job for a sick man." Then he reached into his desk for a book. "This is the other item," he said. "The Manual of Courts Martial of the United States Army, Code of 1806." For a moment he passed a hand across the binding. "This is a valuable book. The over-all rule is that you can lose your commission or save it by that book alone. You live with this—and by it—from now on," and he handed him the manual. "I'm safe in saying Mrs. Alshard will expect you for dinner this evening. You were always her pet junior in the old days at Fort Starke. Senator Bentinck and his spangled circus rider are dining with us."

Cohill glanced sharply at the colonel. Alshard met Cohill's look steadily. "There is a rumor," he said, "that they are to be married, before they sail," and there was a slight emphasis on the word "married." Cohill felt a twist of anger tighten within him, and was instantly surprised at himself. "Yes, sir," he said, "if that'll be all, I'd better be getting on my way."

"Good. See you this evening."

There being no mount available for him, Cohill arranged to go back to Meigg's Wharf on the two o'clock post diligence to San Francisco, stopping first at Wells Fargo's bank in town to deposit the Presidio paymaster's draft to him for two thousand two hundred and fifty-seven dollars back pay and allowances due him while he was detached and reported missing.

In the diligence with the court-martial manual on his lap, an odd thing happened. With an eye casually to glance over it, he held the board ends between each hand and it fell open naturally to the Sixtieth Article of War. For some reason that he was never able to explain to himself, he closed the book again tightly, tapped his knee with it and let it fall open again. Again it opened at the Sixtieth Article of War: "Persons Subject to Military Law—All retainers to the camp and all persons accompanying or serving with the Armies of the United States in the field both within and without the territorial jurisdiction of the United States."

For the third time he tried it. He closed the book and it opened again to the Sixtieth. It was obvious that someone before him had been studying that article and had left the book face downward with the pages turned to it, forcing the binding slightly at the Sixtieth. Cohill concluded that Colonel Alshard had spent some time looking up the potentialities of drastic action according to the book.

The route of the diligence was along Kearney and Montgomery Streets to the turnabout finally at the post office. From the vehicle, Cohill looked out on the slow-moving citizenry: stovepipe hats and claw-hammer coats from South Park; Cantonese in pigtails, and a few broad-hatted sailors from Mare Island Navy Yard; Barbary Coast rangers hooting and dodging in and out in rabid hooliganism; bosomy night-blooming ladies under carriage parasols against the bright afternoon sunlight; scabrous beggars; oily haired Macks; and among them, every raucous accent on the spoken word from Brooklyn to the grating aitchless shriek of far Austrialia.

At Wells Fargo's bank, Cohill got down and went in with his draft. He opened an account with it and drew two hundred dollars in cash for his pocket against the purchase of a horse and equipment. Stepping back from the counter, his head bent slightly as he awkwardly sheafed the bills into his leather pocketbook, his spurred heel struck sharply into a man's foot. "I beg your pardon," and he looked up into a face so pure black that the shadowed light in the offices gave the flesh a sheen of iridescent blue, like the sheen of gun metal. But the man was not Negroid of feature. His lips were as thin as Cohill's, his nose prominent and well arched, his jaw cleanly cut.

He raised his broad-brimmed planter's straw, held it a few inches above and to the right of his head in a gracious gesture, bowed slightly. "Your pardon, sir," he said. "Ramillies Moktir—secretary to Senator Rutherford Bentinck."

Cohill nodded, and moved beyond the man, his pocketbook still in hand, the two hundred dollars half sheafed into it. As he pushed the bills home, he heard the black man say to the counter clerk behind him, "I have a draft for withdrawal signed by Inigo Barras and a covering letter of identification by safe hand from Senator Bentinck."

Then someone pushed between them and Cohill was too far away to hear the clerk's answering words. He turned and went thoughtfully out into the street, where he hailed an empty hackney to take him down to Meigg's Wharf.

The loading operations were in full swing, with a gang on the *Amos Orr* and a gang on the foredeck of the *Clan Cameron* loading cargo at the open hatches. The *Isthmian Queen* and the *Hastings* on the opposite side of the wharf were riding high in the water—almost empty now—and the cargo dump on the dock was considerably depleted since morning. Cohill went aboard the *Clan Cameron* to locate his platoon's work party, standing for a moment at the top of the gangplank. The base of the starboard rail of the quarterdeck above was just at the level of his visor.

He heard a throat cleared heavily and it was Cohill's momentary impression that it was done to attract him. He looked up.

The man at the rail above him wore an impeccably tailored frock coat of dove-gray cloth with a narrow black-velvet collar. He held his right arm slanted out from his shoulder, the hand cupping the knob of an ebony stick. The effect of the posture was theatrical, as if he had consciously posed himself for a portrait photograph. The man's snowy linen ruffed heavily above his canary waistcoat and the wings of his collar pressed high up along his gaunt, gray jaws. He held his head high, giving a slightly grotesque thrust-up effect to his chin. He stood ramrod straight, as if he were drawing his whole body upward from the trouser straps beneath the instep of his varnished boots.

"Sir?" his voice held a heavy resonance. "My respects. You are looking for someone aboard? Possibly I may help you?"

"Compliments, sir. For the platoon from the Presidio," Cohill told him. "I command it—vice Lieutenant Haight," and Cohill gave his name.

"I am Senator Rutherford Bentinck. Your platoon marched off about twenty minutes ago. Cohill? What Cohill would that be? There was a General Cohill——"

"My father, sir. He died four years ago."

"But I knew him *well*, sir! I knew him *well*. Come aboard, sir. Come below with me. It will be an honor to raise a sundown glass with you, Mister Cohill."

Cohill hesitated. He had a distinct conviction that all of this was a rather obvious effort to draw him in; that as Haight's replacement he was being looked over. He decided to do some looking himself, so he crossed to the quarterdeck ladder and scrambled up. His impression from below had been that Bentinck was a tall man, for the rail had reached to his hips only. With some surprise, he saw now that Bentinck was still under what is considered medium height. This fact gave a touch of the ridiculous to his entire dress and manner. "Precede me, sir," the senator indicated the companionway with a flick of his stick, and not until Cohill turned to go down did he step from the raised grating.

The companionway led below into a wide thwartship gallery with stateroom doors in the forward bulkhead. The after bulkhead was arched at the foot of the steps, with doors to close the arch. They were open, so that when Cohill reached the deck below he could see the entire stern cabin spread before him, lit by the afternoon sun blazing upward from the Bay waters.

The senator remained a step up the companionway behind Cohill, motioning him into the cabin to a chair. And when Cohill was seated, he came hurriedly down and sat at once as if again to give denial to his short stature. "A brigadier general of volunteers myself, sir. During the War of the Rebellion," he said, pompously. "In my extreme youth a captain of the great Garibaldi's at Casale and the Ticino crossing. I too—" and he smiled in evident satisfaction, "might well call myself a soldier. Shall we drink—to the Army?" and he beat a sudden staccato tattoo on the tabletop with a heavy seal ring, calling "Ram! *Ram!*"

A door closed somewhere to port in the thwartship passage and there was the sound of footsteps. A moment later a door opened into the stern cabin and the black man of Wells Fargo came in from the pantry beyond. He was in dark alpaca trousers now, bareheaded, and wearing a white, high-necked West Indian serving coat. That Cohill recognized him at once did not embarrass him in the least. He inclined his head with a slight smile as he brought two heavy broad-based ship decanters from the buffet. He returned to bring glasses, heavy linen napkins, lime juice in a mottled opal glass bottle and a shallow silver bowl of shelled pecans. Serving Cohill, he said pleasantly to him, "Secretary to the senator—or steward. As the situation dictates."

The glasses filled, the senator raised his. "To the Army, sir." Bentinck's eyes fascinated Cohill. They were of so light a blue that they gave a first impression of affliction. Heavily browed, they dominated whatever he turned them on. In his early fifties apparently, the senator carried not an ounce of superfluous flesh, and his hands still moved under the tanned muscle pads of youth. The urban formality of his clothing gave the lie to the animality of his whole lithe body.

Cohill acknowledged the toast and they drank. The senator seemed to be considering a personal thought for a moment. Then he raised his napkin, wiped his lips delicately, looked pointedly at his man Ramillies for a moment, then said, "How is General Barras?"

Cohill had the absurd impression that the question was asked only for his own reaction, not for Moktir's. He glanced at the black man and had a sure feeling that there was a surprised question in Moktir's eyes.

"Mister Cohill," the senator said pointedly to his man, "is the son of an old friend of mine, Ram. General Cohill —in Washington during my Army Committee days." He nodded courteously to Cohill. "Inigo Barras," he said, "is an old friend. Traveling with us—indisposed at present with illness." Bentinck looked sharply up at his man. "I suggest you take care of General Barras right now, Ram." Ramillies Moktir hesitated a moment, then nodded and left the cabin.

"I was shocked at young Haight's death this morning, sir," the senator said. "So you replace him?"

"That I do."

"I make no pretense of not resenting this exercise of commandeer on my colonizing expedition, sir!"

"Of that," Cohill said, "I have no part."

"It crowds our facilities abominably."

Cohill said nothing, for there was a sudden unreasoning feeling of outrage upon him at the thought of this little popinjay of a man and the slender dignity of 'Theena, the circus girl, and complete incomprehension as to why he should suddenly elide her name to 'Theena in his mind. He wanted to get out of the cabin, and grasped the arms of the chair to rise.

"But better luck to you, sir, than to poor Haight. Come, let me fill your glass again?" Bentinck reached for a decanter.

"Thank you, no." Cohill stood up and he knew he did it to make the smaller man come to his feet in courtesy. "You have been most hospitable," and he reached for his kepi. The gloved fingers of his hand had not quite touched it when a shot thundered down from the cross passage, the sharp, blatting impact, rolling at once into the full-throated echo of a heavy-calibered gunshot, bounded, compressed, seeking outlet by racketing along the ship's bulkheads.

The senator's arm reached out quickly. His wiry fingers closed on Cohill's wrist in an iron clasp. He half rose from his chair. "Good Lord no," he breathed. *"Ramillies!"* There was a sound of running footsteps and the pantry door opened to his secretary-servant. "Was it from his cabin? Has the General finally done it?"

For a moment the two white men and the black stood there, their eyes in surprised shock, the senator still retaining Cohill's wrist. "I don't know, sir." Then Moktir stepped to the arched entrance as if listening to the complete absence of sound now in the passageway. The senator sprang after him, compelling Cohill to move with him until Cohill angrily jerked himself loose. Moktir was ahead of them, stepping softly down the passage to port. Gingerly he put his fingers to an unlatched cabin door and pushed it open slowly.

A man's body lay jammed in the far corner of the cabin where the heavy shot had flung it backwards from a now overturned stool, the face hidden by the arch of torso which the reflexion of the legs had forced the spine to. An acrid haze of gunsmoke skeined above, woven slightly in a blue web from the air which the opening door had swirled. A forty-four caliber derringer lay under the spread crotch in the shattered shards of a cup and saucer and a greasy stain of liquid, spotted with cooked gobbets of barley. Then a ghastly thing happened. From reflex or some slight movement of the moored ship, the body relaxed its corded tension, gave slowly and sank in upon itself, settling down from its arched posture of exquisite agony, so that Cohill could see the shattered face and head.

The senator pressed Cohill back gently and closed the door. "We have witnessed the final chapter of General Inigo Barras," he said solemnly. "Poor, thwarted devil."

There were footsteps on the deck above—on the companionway. It was two of the ship's officers. The senator said, "I won't detain you, Mister Cohill. You have duties no doubt. There will be an investigation probably. If we have to call you——?"

Then it was that the full conviction struck Cohill that he had been deliberately maneuvered into a position where he could be called upon as witness. You cannot forecast suicide—but you can time murder. He bowed coolly to Bentinck. "I regret that I cannot qualify," he said clearly enough so that the officers heard every word, "for I saw nothing of this." And he climbed back up and left the ship.

He needed a stiff drink when he reached his temporary quarters at the Presidio. While he downed it he heard distantly the three volleys fired over Haight's grave and then the haunting echo of taps on the C trumpet coming down from the post cemetery on the hill rise by Fort Point. Ruminating on Haight's useless demise, Cohill was reminded of the Colonel's warning. Although it was late, he routed out De Canova. The brusk little doctor pursed his lips when Cohill removed the gloves.

"Must've been nasty," he murmured, "but they're well along now. Need air. Keep the gloves on in company but take 'em off whenever you get the chance. And keep flexing those fingers. Gently, but move them. Use them whenever you can. Main thing you'll have to worry about from now on is keeping 'em supple. And the scars of course. That grease isn't going to help anymore.

Get air to them and use 'em. It'll hurt." With which reassuring edict, the doctor dismissed Cohill.

At a quarter to eight that evening, in a borrowed helmet and shell jacket with aiguilette, Cohill picked his way around the witch-black parade grounds toward Colonel Alshard's lighted quarters, carrying a nonissue hand gun in the pocket of his riding cape and feeling somewhat embarrassed by the fact.

There was a carriage drawing up at a walk from the post gates.

As he was placing his cape and helmet on the table in the rear of the hall, he was conscious of Colonel Alshard's white-coated dog-robber answering a second ring at the door behind him. Down the hallway the man opened the door again and he saw Athena come into the golden pool of lamplight. Seeing her, he felt his entire body pull taut from his thighs.

She was in white satin, a full-skirted evening gown, draped at the shoulders in a blue velvet cape, an exquisite breath of the outside world of smart cities against the bleak and lonely Presidio night. Her golden hair held a tiny jeweled ornament that fired deep in the lamplight. In the moment that Cohill recognized the countess from the morning gone, his breath drew in against the instinctive vital constriction within him and the hungry tumult of the starved months past gripped like a claw. Then a vicious rage of animal jealousy shot through him as Senator Bentinck came in behind her, patently possessive, his shortness covered by his raised silk hat held above his head.

CHAPTER FOUR

COHILL BOWED TO ATHENA, stiffly conscious that as a woman she was stirring him deeply and knew it. The senator was busy paying his respects elsewhere, and in the moment that they had, Cohill said, "May I say that you are very beautiful this evening?"

"For pity's sake," she touched him lightly with her fan. "Don't speak your words off by rote. I will not bite you." And there was no faint trace of coquetry in the gesture or in her words; a forthright effort, rather, to put him at his ease.

"I have not talked to a white woman in over two years," he said, "until you—this morning. It takes getting used to again." His voice was husky. "It takes gentling down. What do I call you?"

"I was christened Athena Havilford, which means nothing to you, obviously. The Havilfords—my father, my brother and myself—were the most celebrated equestrian team in the circus world. We bred our horses as well as performed them. Since I have been alone, I have had some personal success myself as Athena. I think I told you how much *success* this morning." Her eyes hesitated as a note of self mockery crept into her voice, and he knew suddenly that she was doing exactly what she had done before—presenting herself as what she was and then deriding the fact. Some inner turmoil of soul demanded that she deride and mock herself.

"Don't *do* that to yourself," he said sharply, his white-gloved hand half outstretched in an earnest gesture. "There is no cause to do it—and it does not become you. You are obviously a woman of breeding, entitled to walk in pride. Walk then in pride. Without self-belittlement."

She stared at him with rising hostility. "I do not think that I have said or done anything that would give you the right to speak this frankly to me." Then she turned her eyes slightly from him. "The way of my living is of my own choosing. I am committed to it fully. Therefore no one has the privilege of questioning it."

"Is it possible," he asked bluntly, "that you are in need of someone to help you, and that you are denying the necessity even to yourself?"

For a moment again, as she had that morning, she watched him intently, searching him out, questioning his ability to understand. Her level glance reflected infinitely more feminine maturity than her years actually gave her.

There was Navy arriving now; the commodore from Mare Island, his aide, and their gaunt wives, with Acting Mayor Turnage of San Francisco surrounded by his three-hundred-pound lady, giggling in poinsetta silk. Side-burned Captain Duncommun of the garrison troop stomped in with his two sharp-elbowed daughters, grim Miss Duncommun and the younger Miss Ermintrude Duncommun, not yet quite turned forty.

Cohill had only a moment more with Athena, for Bentinck was crossing back to them from Abigail Alshard and the colonel— making his pompous greetings to the other guests. Earnestly and softly Cohill murmured, "You have told me of your trouble in Mexico and indicated that your fortunes are broken. You are a young widow—tragically. An attractive woman in a world that is not too kind. If it is in your mind that you must defend yourself to me against the talk which you must know would assail any woman dramatically situated as you are, then disabuse yourself of the necessity. For I will not accept gossip where you are concerned—" then deep fury stifling him—"but if I was forced to accept it I would kill the man who caused the truth of it, if the truth was contrary to your wishes!"

When he had said it, she closed her eyes tightly for a moment, the tip of her tongue pressed between her lips. In that moment there was a desperate shadow of helplessness upon her face—as of a wound gone too deep for words. Then, mechanically from another time and another manner of living, she touched his arm again with the tip of her folded fan. Fending him off lightly, but with slight pressure at the same time that carried the faint suggestion of knife-point warning. "You could be—a very disturbing man, sir," she said softly, but he knew beyond any question that were they alone, he could have reached in that moment and taken her blindly in his arms and she would have clung to him in sobbing desperation. So sure was the knowledge upon him, that he was trembling with it.

"You would do me great honor if you would dine with me tomorrow evening."

"That," she said coldly, "is quite impossible. I am restricted to the *Clan Cameron*—except for the arrangements I have made for Turk here at the Presidio."

"I don't understand. How restricted? By what?"

"When I married in Europe, I lost my citizenship. I am an alien in my own country—not allowed to land because my husband fought against the Government of Mexico," and then most unnecessarily, "You would do well, sir, to seek the companionship of some woman less encumbered."

All through dinner under the shrill clack of tongues of the Misses Duncommun, Cohill found himself more deeply committed to the girl; felt a complete selflessness for her within him that he was unable to define in essence. This was the last thing in the world to do under his present orders, entangle himself personally in any way; but as he watched Athena covertly, he knew that he was powerless not to, that he already had committed himself in some deep, honest core of his being. For as he listened to the dominating pomposity of Bentinck, all animal jealousy drained out of him because it became utterly impossible for him to accept Bentinck in the garments that rumor draped him in.

When the ladies withdrew, Bentinck's voice carried heavily on over the brandy and the cigars while Cohill sat lost in his own thinking. "I am going into that vast and neglected Colorado country, as appointive Territorial Governor on a sacred mission to colonize and develop its rich resources and to bring competent civil government to it, sir." The senator's voice rose arrogantly. "Two ships are barely enough for my purpose as it is. With your supplies and your detachment added——"

"Forgive my bluntness," Colonel Alshard interrupted, "but unless telegraphic orders come through from Washington expressly forbidding it, Mister Cohill's relief detachment will go with you, under my right to commandeer space for it. And it will go as soon as you possibly can sail, now that the Second Cavalry is no longer an effective force in the Territory."

Senator Bentinck thrust his chin up angrily. "Normally," he said, "the Department of California is commanded by a brigadier general, is it not?" He waited for no answer. "If then," the senator said coldly, "your promotion does not materialize, colonel, don't be unduly surprised."

Cohill whipped around angrily and stared at Bentinck. Commodore Blase half opened his mouth and snapped it tight shut again in fury at the churlishness of the political threat. Colonel Alshard kept his eyes steadily on the senator's eyes, his own veiled in contempt. Dead silence fell across the candle-lit table, and under its echoing impact Cohill knew the full implication of his orders for the first time. With the power that this popinjay held through his contacts in distant Washington, any move against him could undoubtedly cost an officer his career. The power of the whispered word at three thousand miles of distance.

A splenetic loathing for the position this placed the colonel and himself in rose like bile within Cohill, and he was incapable of not giving it voice. "As the junior officer present," he said clearly, "with infinitely less to lose—I consider your remark contemptible." He rose, and the scrape of his chair was harsh and loud in the silence. Cohill inclined his head toward his colonel. "With your permission, sir," he said quietly, and bowing to the others, he left.

CHAPTER FIVE

COHILL WAS IN THE STABLE AREA at five the next morning against the Presidio's five-thirty reveille, looking over the platoon horses in their stalls by lantern light.

There were twenty-seven men in his relief platoon. Three squads, the two sergeants and the trumpeter. The three squad leaders were eight-year corporals, which is solid disciplinary structure. Platoon Sergeant Satterlee was a long-service noncom, but Ohms, the guide sergeant, was comparatively young for his stripes. Musician Lance Corporal Weigandt was an adolescent pinwheel with pimples, but he could lip the C trumpet like Gabriel. All but eleven of the troopers had been in garrison at Yuma and Fort Mojave on tours of duty before, had made the sea trip down to the port of entry in the Gulf and the Blood River trip up to the isolated posts, and loathed it like dysentery. But there was more than that wrong with the men in the sullen early morning feel of them as they stood to. The line twanged with deep-cut anger.

"What's wrong with the men, Sergeant Satterlee?"

Old Satterlee looked sideways at Cohill, knew it useless to lie, and so straddled the fence. "Wrong, sir?"

"Yes, *wrong*," Cohill said. "That's what I said—*wrong*. Do you want to tell me, Satterlee, or keep it slow-boiling inside? We have a long trip to the Rio. Shall we get to know each other or play it blind?"

"I dunno, lieutenant." Satterlee shook his head vaguely. "We was all below decks when it happened, but the word says

Lieutenant Haight was knifed. And these men don't take knives from nobody. The civilian gang boss Boldoni carries a stiletto blade. That's been seen plenty by all of us. But when the U.S. marshal's men come to the dock and made a search, Boldoni's got a red neckrag but he don't have no knife. So they let him go. Couldn't do else. No evidence.'"

Cohill moved the platoon out with the first convoy of supplies for Meigg's Wharf, studying them closely still. The usual lot of regulars—lost men except for a brighteyed youngster or two. Men with no place in the world to go except to the Army. Cut a cross-section and you would find every degree of failure from the outside—jailbirds, rum pots, wife-beaters, and plain pernicious misfits. But hammer them firmly into the system and they were home; put them together in disciplined unity and a protective self-respect came back to them that no one among them did not feel in some corner of his tattered soul. The last chance of all the doubtful chances life had given them—the Army. The one hope of redemption, if they ever thought of it that way, for enlistment is the only contract in life that gives back personal honor to a lost man. You can betray a woman, cheat a friend, desert a child, and fight back to a semblance of decency and forgetfulness. But for fifty cents a day—you can never run from the memory that you committed yourself to the United States as a self-respecting man.

The convoy got to Meigg's Wharf shortly after seven o'clock, before any loading had started on the two ships. With the sunrise, there was half an hour of blinding golden light on the whole broad stretch of the Bay, then fog poured in through the Gate and spread like viscous liquid, shrouding Fort Point, blanketing out Alcatraz Island and banking thick in the *Clan's* upper rigging until it was solid gray over the ship and the dock, wisping down to rasp men's thoats, requiring lanterns in the holds.

They unloaded the first supply convoy and sent the wagons back for the next load. Below decks Satterlee read Cohill into the work already done on the stalls.

"Tailboards." Sergeant Satterlee lifted one on its hinges. "That's the secret. If a horse can back up and sit himself down to brace against weather, he'll ride through a hurricane. And for exercise we got to prance 'em in place, stir 'em up at least once a day."

As he said it, there was a hollow rumble above decks, booted feet clattering across the well-deck. Cohill stepped back under the open hatch and saw some of Boldoni's civilian gang breaking out hoisting lines, spreading a cargo net at the hatch above. He heard a voice shout "Come on soldier—you're blocking"; heard Sergeant Ohm's voice yell back sharply "Hold that, guinea-nose!" Cohill sprang up the hatchladder fast. When he reached the well-deck, he saw Ohms and Boldoni squared off to each other.

"Pull a knife, yella belly," Ohms jeered. "Pull it!" The sergeant walked toward Boldoni slowly, his whole young body braced forward, the muscles corded tense under his faded blue shirt, the three buck stripes bright yellow on his arms. "Naw," Ohms shook his head in contempt, "not you—not where a man can see ya! What'd you do yesterday, throw it overside after you kilt the lootenent? Look —" Ohms pointed a rigid finger up at the foggy crossyards and the maze of rigging "—that's where they're gonna find you, wop-nose—jiggin' on air—like the book says!" and he made the rope gesture to his own throat in vibrant, taunting anger "—by the neck, *until you're bug-eyed dead!*"

"Break it up—both of you!" Cohill stepped between them. Boldoni hulked above him, topping him by three or four inches. "I run things when Carracoe's drunk!" he shouted.

"You run nothing—with my men," Cohill told him. Boldoni took a step toward him. "The *new* officer, eh," and he reached slowly to finger-dust Cohill's left shoulder strap in contempt. Cohill knew he had to take him and he knew he didn't have the strength in his damaged hands to do it. So he shot a lightning hand heel to Boldoni's wishbone and caught a spur rowel in his right ankle. Boldoni crashed to the deck with the breath torn out of him. "Get up now," Cohill told him, "and show me to Major Carracoe's quarters."

Under the troop's laughter and his own men's snickering, Boldoni's eyes wavered. Then he got up, hesitated for a moment, and jerked his head toward the afterhouse.

There was a galley across the forward end of it and a passage through aft with two staterooms off each side and a narrow companionway leading to the deck below. Cohill pushed his booted foot to the door of the first port-side cabin, slamming it open.

Major Carracoe lay face up in his fouled berth, the drink in him ebbed full to blank-eyed enervation, conscious but clouded deep in his mind, parched raw with alcohol. "Burned hands!" he muttered. "The curse of Druon Antigone! *Cut the hands off!*"

In Cohill's mind, there was no thought of covering for this degradation of rank—nothing beyond his own necessity to force the immediate issue. There might be questions raised as to legality under the right of commandeer, but there would be no question, in fact, once he established what he deemed to be necessary for the exercise of duties of his own detachment in transit. And he intended to establish the fact on the basis that the civilians and Bentinck's raw militiamen notwithstanding, United States troops would take what was essential to the accomplishment of their mission, and they would take it in reasonable personal comfort.

For a moment Cohill stood at the foot of the berth, watching the man's eyes for recognition and reaction. Carracoe's arm dropped from the berth edge, the hand flobbering for the neck of the demijohn on the deck. Cohill kicked at the hand, kneed the arm to the bunk and smashed the jug on the brass port rim. Then he threw open all the lockers and drawers and shattered the five bottles of de Kuyper that he found. He pocketed six boxes of cartridges and emptied the major's two hand guns. He wrenched the key from the inside of the door lock and stood chucking it in his gloved hand. "We'll discuss that militia major's leaf of yours when you're sober enough to grace it," he said, and he went out and locked Carracoe in.

The fog smoked in thick all day, but the platoon handled seven wagon convoys in spite of it and by late afternoon they had the back of the supply loading broken and the stalls padded to take the horse herd aboard. Watching his own work closely and Bentinck's people narrowly to spot trouble before it broke again, Cohill had no sight of Bentinck nor of Athena all that day. About four o'clock, when the first convoy of ammunition wagons turned into the dock from the Presidio, three officers in frogged overcoats and side arms got off the first of them. The board of inquiry on Lieutenant Haight's death. Old Captain Duncommun, side-burned Captain Oettinger, the post quartermaster, and the sixty-year-old First Lieutenant Grattan, topographical engineers—with a scrabbly white beard so long that it covered the collar of his overcoat and the first two frogs. At their request Cohill showed the board the approximate spot where from offshore in the *Lucy's* longboat he had seen young Haight go down under the first blow, visualizing for them the cargo heap, now almost entirely loaded off the dock onto the two ships for the Colorado, and the bollard Haight's head had struck when he was leg-flung into it. The quartermaster captain stooped to what was left of the supply dump, examining the government markings. "Has the expedition loaded any field pieces, Cohill?"

"No, sir. Not that I have seen."

Captain Oettinger snorted. "What do they need modified Whitworth field artillery ammunition for then, without guns? Culpable waste! This stuff's been stored since Appomattox—dead surplus—but could we get it across the Mississippi for Army use? No indeed! It takes political influence for that!"

Half a dozen of Boldoni's men came off the ship and gathered idly around the three board members, to watch the proceedings. Cohill looked sharply into their faces wondering what bait

Bentinck had used to lure them three thousand miles west into the criminal disorganization of this expedition.

As Cohill went up the forward gangplank, Wertenbacker—one of the men of Clegg's squad—pointed to the three overcoated officers on the dock. "Whitewash board on Lootenant Haight," he growled in disgust, and the man next to him grunted, "Line of duty at the hands of person or persons, unknown *like hell!*" Then their eyes wiped Cohill's as if they had been caught in something shameful, not merely the impersonal sullenness of overworked men to a new officer.

Cohill felt their constriction so strongly that he made a quick visual check as a netload of small-arms ammunition swung up from the Presidio wagons. Wertenbacker, Oelrichs, Font and Gilhoolie were on the well-deck, with Corporal Clegg himself on the boom whip handhoist. Cohill stepped over to the forward hatch and looked down. All three hatches below him were open—straight down in the wavering lantern light to the choke-loaded bottom hold. Foley and Dressler of Clegg's squad were just below on the open hatch lip of the stall deck, swung slightly out, one hand each to a stanchion, looking upward in the yellow glare of a lantern, waiting to hook in the loaded net of ammunition.

There was loose cargo cluttering the hatch head—a limp net of barreled flour, dropped where the hoist had swung it, crated saddles and four ordnance cases of carbines, one topping the other and standing high in a second limp net loosely hooked in. Coiled hoist rope fouled all of it with lines leading up to booms in the thick, lantern-washed fog above and snarled lines snaking down into the lower holds.

As Cohill stood there, the heavy ammunition boxes swung over the deck on Clegg's boom whip and smashed into the carbine cases. *"Look out below!"* and then everybody was falling back, scrambling out of the way. The four carbine cases tottered over, buckled one on the other inside their net like a crushed accordion, and shot into the open hatch, plummeting below like chain shot.

For a breath, the fog-curtained hatch was empty, an open pit yellowed by lantern light, fumed in swirling mist with the thunder of the splintering ordnance cases echoing up hollowly through it. Then on the lash of the smoking downhaul rope, a man's body vomited up out of the hatchway, twisting in frantic agony, diving up neck-hung to the block like a suffocating swimmer in the fog, snapping double as the counterbalance of the carbines struck onto the lower hold and slacked the line. The rope-snarled legs drew back at the knees, drew up at the hips with the anguished reflex of the groin muscles, then thrust down on the empty air and hung flag-footed limp.

There was dead silence, until someone shouted "Boldoni!" Then the civilian work gang broke as cattle break in blind trampling fear and the deck thundered with the staccato of their bodies clattering to get away. They choked the head of the forward gangplank, flooded to the starboard rail, scrabbled blindly back aft.

Sergeant Ohms sprang out of the hatch and faced the fear-whipped crowd as soon as Boldoni's body stopped thrashing, scurrying a few feet after the panicked civilian gang like an animal, half crouched at the knees, his lethal arms flailing the air, his voice a strident snarl. "Go on, look at him, you chicken-gutted sock-heads!" and Ohms flung an arm back, his finger pointing rigidly at the hanging body. "I told him he'd hang—*so he's hanging!*"

Ohms turned from them then and saw Cohill. At the same time the faces of the other men of the platoon's deck detail turned toward Cohill in a unified movement, distorted by fog and lantern light.

Just as surely as he stood there, Cohill knew that Ohms had set the trap. Rigged the counterweight of carbines, lured Boldoni below decks to truss and gag him for the noose, when opportunity offered. As Cohill faced Ohms now, a whipstring of a man and a horse soldier to the dudgeon, he knew that Ohms knew he knew. Just for a second, then, there was the light of cold-blooded murder in Ohms' eyes before he went on the defensive.

"Remember, you ain't got a knife in your ribs too, sir!" Then animal fury took the sergeant again, shattered his surface shell of discipline and he whipped half-around toward the civilians—"and you gutter bums ain't forgettin' either that a knife in a blue shirt pays off with a hangin' like it's written to pay in the book—as long as I wear one to m'own stinkin' back!"

"Cut him down, Ohms!" Cohill shouted the man to silence.

The ship's captain, Houget, was pushing through, with his mate, Moxley. Captain Duncommun and Captain Oettinger had come up the after gangplank. Boldoni's men were still crowded well back of the hatch head, muttering openly now as the starch began to stiffen back into them.

Moxley knelt to the body, pulling at the strands of the rope caught about it. "He ain't rightly tied, Captain, he's just looped and snarled up." Moxley looked up at Captain Houget. "Seen a cargo hoist fling a man oncet clear over the main yardarm that-away, when he got caught up in the downhaul."

Captain Duncommun said, "How did it happen, Cohill?"

"You saw all that I saw, sir." Cohill met the board president's eye. "It's the gang boss Boldoni," he said. "I can't add any details to it, but if he killed Haight, he damn well hanged for it, sir!" Then he looked over the captain's shoulder, straight at Ohms. He held the sergeant's eyes for a cold moment until Ohms' eyes wavered. "Get on with the work, Ohms," he said.

CHAPTER SIX

COHILL WATCHED OHMS NARROWLY as he pushed the loading hard up to the break-off for late evening mess. There was a primeval savagery in the man that was twisted by his surface constraint of discipline so that he was not quite a brute and not quite a civilized man. Alone with Boldoni in the lower hold, he could have kicked the gang boss to death, bale-hooked him or throttled him with his bare hands—but not Sergeant Ohms. He was a killer with three cavalry stripes to his arms, and yet with a macabre respect for the saving grace of the book. And for murder the book specified the rope.

As he watched the sergeant, Cohill was aware that Ohms was watching him and he knew that sooner or later Ohms would have to speak him. Ohms did, half petulantly, half angrily, when he couldn't stand it any longer. He made a point of working over close to Cohill and then standing for a moment, looked at him.

"Well, Ohms?"

"The lieutenant knows I did it. I seen it in your face."

Men like Ohms are not types. They are individuals. There is only one rule in handling them. Take them fast or they take you. "Put it in writing and sign it," Cohill said, "and I'll see you tried for it. What is it? Bad conscience?"

Ohms' mouth dropped open in surprise, then a sly shadow crossed his eyes and Cohill realized that the man thought he meant it, thought Cohill was stupid enough to be asking for a statement. Ohms' voice vibrated with fury. "They got fifty half-pratted militia soldiers on this bucket alone, sir, and fifty in the civilian gang! Four to one against us. Count the fifty more on the *Amos Orr* makes seven to one. Them's odds. But they seen what the price of a knife is. They know now!"

Boldoni's gang had knocked off work and were pouring up from below to go off into town. The decks were suddenly full of them—white blobbed faces in the fog staring at the platoon's work detail—ringing them in—with the sloppy uniforms of the territorial militiamen interspersed among them. Somebody shouted "Yellow-legged hangmen!" but before the threat could spread into action, Ohms took over again. He flailed his way from Cohill's side to the starboard rail and sprang up on it, his brass rowels spinning in the lantern light. "Alright you crudheads! Step up! Who's next? There's plenty of rope!" Cohill shouted, "Hold it, Ohms! You, Clegg, put a fixed sentry on this forward gangplank," and he walked slowly toward the angry crowd that Ohms had driven back, his arms outspread to herd them back until he reached the forward corner of the afterhouse. "Up to here," he told them, "is United States Government property. Keep off it. Keep away from that forward hatch at all times. Use the after gangplank. Clegg, put a sentry here where I'm standing."

"Yeh?" somebody shouted. "What'll ya do if we don't?"

Corporal Clegg posted Wertenbacker at the gangplank head, buckling on his belt and hand gun. He was crossing the deck with Gilhoolie to post him at the afterhouse.

"What'll they do—shoot, mister?"

Cohill whipped around and faced the gang again. "If they don't," he said clearly, "I will."

There was a long moment then, until the men on the outer edge of the crowd shuffled sullenly and began to file down the after gangplank. Only then did Cohill turn to Ohms. "You start anything more with these people and I'll have those stripes off your sleeve so fast they'll smoke!"

Ohms' eyes wavered slightly and then flamed full with the man's innate viciousness. Softly out of the side of his mouth he snarled, "You better get along with me, lieutenant! You're gonna need me."

Cohill stepped up to him fast, forcing Ohms to give a pace. He watched the man's eyes closely, until the brute glaze faded from them. "You want that official, Ohms? You want me to hear it full voice? Does it stand—for your stripes?"

"No, sir." Ohms' eyes wavered again. "It ... don't ... stand."

Cohill bought the evening paper and read it by lantern light riding an empty wagon up to the Presidio.

SUICIDE OF INIGO BARRAS
CONNECTED WITH SECOND CAVALRY MASSACRE

Late yesterday afternoon the notorious "General" Inigo Barras killed himself in his cabin aboard the *Clan Cameron,* loading for the Colorado at Meigg's Wharf. He was wanted on a Justice department warrant for violation of the Neutrality Treaty with Mexico and unauthorized negotiation with the Mescalero and Jicarillo headmen in the Arizona country of New Mexico Territory. The United States Marshal in San Francisco has had information since January that Barras was making illegal tribal contact in the central Arizona country and could be expected to work his way north across the Colorado into California. Informed sources blame Barras' grandiose promises to the tribes for the present general uprising and the resulting massacre of the Second Cavalry column on the Gila River as reported yesterday.

Until the Neutrality Commission stopped him two years ago, Inigo Barras commanded the Legion of Liberation, a marauding force of freebooters that controlled most of northern Mexico, a brigade of which is, from time to time, still reported as operating in Sonora State.

In the agreement then made with the Republic of Mexico, Barras was given safe conduct to Tampa. He was suspected of taking most of his military loot with him, abandoning ten of his Legion's officers to be executed at Guadalajara by the Mexican authorities, among them the luckless Count Paul of Wurtenberg, whose attractive widow is also a passenger on the *Clan Cameron.*

When questioned as to the circumstances of the suicide, Senator Rutherford Bentinck, who heads the Colorado Expedition, stated that he had found Barras destitute and in broken health in Mazatlán when the *Clan Cameron* put in at that port on its way north from Panama and that he had given him asylum aboard under the name of H. Docher to protect Barras from possible assassination at the hands of his disgruntled followers. This was the name carried on the *Clan Cameron's* passenger lists and it was unknown until yesterday even to Captain Houget of the *Clan* that the ship carried Inigo Barras, as Barras had made no attempt to land and the port authorities had therefore not examined his papers.

Cohill folded the paper. It was patent to him that the reporter who had written the account was not satisfied in some way and was telling his readers that he wasn't, but the point of dissatisfaction was as nebulous as Cohill's reaction to the shooting had been yesterday. Suspicion—not fact.

Fog and darkness drowned the entire post in damp salt rime. When the empty wagons drew in at the stable area, Sergeant Satterlee took Cohill inside and indicated the platoon's division of troop organizational equipment: farrier's tools, saddlery spare parts, vet medicines, stable gear and kegged shoes. "In here, sir, along this wall. In the lean-to and the separate shed behind, where the lady keeps the trick stallion."

"Where what?"

"Post commander's orders, sir. She exercises the stallion up here."

"March the detail to mess, sergeant. Get the guard squad's gullion in pannikins—to take down aboard."

Cohill stood for a moment in the horse-warm stable after the men had gone. Then he went to the back door and opened it on the heavy fog outside. The shed was twenty feet behind, with lantern light yellowing its one high window. He went quickly across and pulled open the door, heard 'Theena's voice in the gloom beyond. "Steady, Turk!" and the throat whistle of the stallion.

"Cohill," he called to her. "Are you quite mad? We don't let females even cross the parade ground after nightfall on Army posts unless they are under officer escort. Do you want to be found at reveille stripped and pegged out stiff with a hoof-knife in your throat?"

She came out of the stall, her divided riding skirt whipping in annoyance, horse brush in hand. Her hair was wisped slightly under her tricorn, damp from her exertion.

"I'll have a trooper detailed to groom your mount." He jerked his head to the stall.

The stallion went up on his halter at the sound of Cohill's unaccustomed voice and snorted viciously.

"And have your trooper maimed?" she asked. "Yor...boy...yor," she called softly as the Arab high-stepped, veering left to swing his off eye to see, jerking his head around, his wet nostrils flaring.

"If you're the horsewoman you appear to be, you ought to know a woman has no business trying to handle a stallion. I mean—"

"I know quite well what you mean," she said evenly. "Shall we drop the discussion? I've handled Turk since he was foaled."

He felt the blood beat in his cheekbones; watched her toss the brush to a bench-top and step into the stall to the oat chute.

"I'll do that!" he told her and brushed by her, but she clamped a quick hand to his sleeve. "Get out of this stall! He doesn't know you!" She stamped her booted foot in anger. The stallion straining up again, screaming, threw himself savagely toward them, and, crouched, Cohill shielded her with his own body as the hoof-shattered splinters showered them. Then, as the Arab tugged up on his halter to strike again, Cohill dragged the girl out by one wrist and flung her from the stall headlong, diving after her as the stallion's iron heels bit close into the sideboards behind.

Athena half hurdling, tipped the bench with her boot heel, spinning it fair across Cohill's shins, throwing him full over it. They went down heavily in the straw with Cohill twisting desperately in mid-air in an attempt to keep the full weight of his body from smashing down onto hers. For a moment they lay sprawled breathless in the warm silence of the dimly lit shed, unable to move until reflex female panic tore frantically through her in a desperate spasm to be free of his inert weight. He caught at her thrashing shoulders to steady her—and he was stark with the sudden turmoil of their bodies writhing together. She whipped her head furiously from side to side, lashing his face with the warm musk of her hair, her throat bubbling softly with a half-fearful whimper, and he saw terror in her eyes—"For God's sake don't hold onto me!" and she tore free of him, struggling to her knees, her hands clutching the rip in her blouse. Then she laughed—in a short, barking fury of laughter. Personal to her alone in a way that shut him completely out —and the sound of it was horrid.

"Stop that!" Cohill told her, and he twisted on his own knees and clapped a gloved hand over her half-opened mouth to smother the sound. Above his hand her eyes stared at him with the humiliation of embarrassment. Then she crinkled them tightly shut as if a spasm of pain had torn through her.

She braced herself on the overturned bench and stood up. There was the ridiculous sound of the Arab unconcernedly munching oats.

"Could you have any faint conception of what actually happened in Guadalajara two years ago—" and the soft whisper of her voice was wet with unshed tears—"I would not have to excuse myself to you for playing the hysterical girl. I loathe myself, but I cannot help it. Forgive me for my stupidity," she begged him earnestly, "but I cannot bear to be touched—"

She backed to the shed door, brought up against it, her hands behind her, her eyes bleakly on Cohill's. Suddenly she flicked the latch and turned as if from evil, flinging the door open to its opaque plug of smoking fog, fleeing into it.

Cohill snatched for the lantern, followed her out on the run and lost all orientation as soon as the fog closed about him, until halting, he forced his mind to visualize the area from memory. He held the lantern high, so that its light drenched his head and shoulders in golden light. " 'Theena!"

Off to his right, beyond the corral fence, he heard a sentry challenge the relief. There was no other sound in the fog-muffled darkness. He moved to the fence and began to follow it on down toward the post gates. Once again he called to the girl when it seemed to him that he heard the sound of light footsteps ahead of him. But there was no answer that time either.

Then abruptly, melting the shroud of fog, there was the sudden wash of lantern light under the guardhouse ramada and the lamp of a hackney carriage with a long-coated jehu standing at the horses' heads. Cohill saw the girl running ahead of him then, saw the sheen of light on the damp-beaded nap of Bentinck's stovepipe hat, on the hilt of the officer of the guard's saber—old white-bearded Lieutenant Grattan.

"Ah!" Bentinck said heavily, "we've just sent an orderly to the stables to look for you, Athena." He took her hands in both of his, but she withdrew them at once. "You're frozen, my dear," and he handed her into the rig. Not handed actually, for the senator's hands were merely outstretched toward her as she flung herself into the carriage, as it seemed to Cohill, in a blind effort to get away.

CHAPTER SEVEN

WITH THE WORD PASSED BY MOXLEY that the *Clan Cameron* would sail when the fog lifted, Cohill worked his detail until midnight and slept aboard on the stall deck with the guard detachment. With the Bay waters of the Pacific lazily cradling the moored ship under Cohill, his mind flashed the long way east to the Atlantic along that tenuous three-thousand-mile pathway of empire, the rugged outposts of which had been his chosen place of duty for many years of pressure on the hostiles. A railroad traced all the way over the north central part of the country now, but the broad sweep of the southwestern deserts had swollen far below its steel tourniquet and burst into ulceration to spread savage reprisal once again upon the White Eyes, and against that present fact, no individual mattered. Neither young Haight, uselessly dead in youth, nor his own professional future beyond the constraint of his present orders. He forced his mind consciously to drift in vengeful fury for his cut-up Regiment.

He could see the disastrous Gila River fight starkly in his mind's eye as only a frontier officer can ever see it. The final, desperate lines, in the pre-dawn half-light of Apache reveille, with the dead bunkered out stiff around the last circle of living resistance, dirty-handed and clutching. With a handful of the living crouched close, to sell out high. Far off, the shriek of a wounded horse from yesterday's action, thrashing legs snarled in its own white entrails. The slough-breathing of the wounded in the pit, holding on in agony, as they always did, with the ghastly will to live against all hope of life. One man begging the eternal night through—to be shot by his bunkie. Until he damn well had to be.

Then he realized what he was actually doing: blanketing out his mind from its desires, and he realized that all evening he had kept himself nose-close to the job in hand like an anchorite in enforced effort to thrust 'Theena out of his consciousness. She came back to him now, a soft hand of tenderness, and he lay stark and sweating with her presence full upon him. Involuntarily he clenched his fists and was joltingly reminded of the doctor's edict. Deliberately he set himself to a methodical one-finger-at-a-time exercise, grateful for the distraction the pain and required concentration offered.

With the fog still down at dawn, Satterlee's detail led the horse herd down to Meigg's and by seven o'clock they started to load the animals. To mount himself, Cohill got a carryall to take him and his horse gear up to Bustanoboys Auction Stables, after noon mess, and he bought a three year old. Bought the animal on instinct that his blood lines had not been appreciated by the people who had tried to handle him before. For you can have that feeling for horses, that they have been affronted and deeply insulted; that they have to come home to their own kind, to be content.

Nervy for exercise, Cohill rode the animal at a close-held, skittering walk through the cluttered hill streets, schooling him to his own control, to Montgomery, and tied him at the hitchrail in front of Wells Fargo's bank while he went in. To the clerk he said, "I'm leaving town unexpectedly. I want a sight draft for my deposit of two days ago."

The clerk opened one of the board-covered account books, and fingered the columns until he came to his name. "For all of it, sir? For the entire amount? That's a lot of money. In *one* draft did you say, sir?"

"In one draft," Cohill nodded. There was a panic shout in the street outside. Cohill turned his head to the windows and saw his horse lashing his hooves murderously at the sidewalk crowd. "Draw the draft—I'll be back," and he ran out. He reached the animal and swung with him on the halter into the center of the narrow street. "Stea*day*...ho-down, boy...ho!" And because there was no other sure way, he flung himself into the saddle and gathered him in close hand. The mount went up on his coiled hind quarters as the shrieks of the scampering crowd tore at his sensitive ears. He pirouetted twice on his hind legs and came down braced and trembling to Cohill's hand, to Cohill's insistent voice. He held for a moment.

Cohill saw the bank's clerk in the doorway, signaled to him. The man stepped out warily with the draft, handed it up, and Cohill stuffed it in his pocket. Then he gave the horse his head and he broke full down the open street to satiate his strung nerves.

In the lower town, Cohill walked him across the flats and through the shore gates of Meigg's Wharf. Up at the end, along-side the *Clan Cameron,* Sergeant Satterlee was waiting for him.

"Commanding officer is come aboard, sir. Inspecting the stall deck. Fog's breaking at the Gate. Ship's sailing with the evening tide, sir."

Cohill dismounted and gave Satterlee the bridle. "Load him aboard—but watch him, he can be a prima donna."

"Not no more'n the lady's trick stallion, sir. We just got him aboard."

Colonel Alshard met Cohill at the hatchhead, walked him apart, forward. He stood looking at Cohill closely for a moment. "I'm worried about ventilation in the stable deck," he said. "You'll have to watch that closely if you strike heavy weather and they have to batten down."

"Yes, sir," Cohill said, because he knew the colonel's remark was superficial and there was no answer expected to it. For a moment MacClendon Alshard stood looking absently across the Bay waters into the thinning fog that was burning off now in a golden wash of the westering sun. Then he said, "Cohill, I don't like any of this. I've had another long session with the United States marshal. He's a policeman with a policeman's suspicions, but I must respect his thinking. Just as it was his theory that young Haight was killed to deprive your detachment of its officer, so it is his theory now that Inigo Barras was never aboard this ship. That the man, listed as Docher, was actually Docher. That whatever happened, he was presented as Barras in order to draw a red herring across that Justice Department warrant. You can't arrest a dead man, but if a wanted man is believed to be dead, the chase falls off and gives him complete freedom of operation." The colonel reached to an inner pocket and produced an envelope. "If the marshal is right, you may have Barras in your hair yet."

Cohill read:

First Lieutenant F. Cohill 2[d] Cav. will proceed from this Headquarters on temporary duty via *Clan Cameron* and Colorado River steamers in command of troops allocated and will effect the relief of the garrisons at Fort Yuma and Fort Mojave in accordance with Standing Orders this Headquarters, attached hereto. As senior officer present on the Colorado, he will exercise all administrative duties, including court-martial jurisdiction, and will take command of all United States troops in the area until the relief is effected. This temporary duty in transit being discharged, subject officer will rejoin 2[d] Cav. in pursuance of original orders.

"Are there any questions, Cohill?"

"No, sir."

"I want you to understand fully what it is that I am being forced to do to you, Cohill," the Colonel said carefully. "I am untying you from all command, control and communication from all higher authority for an indefinite period of time—against a hostile situation of which I have very sketchy intelligence and against other conditions that are at best highly questionable." He made a slight, involuntary gesture to include the ship.

"Yes, sir."

"I would not relish being placed in such a situation myself, for in a sense," Alshard said, "I am placing in your hands the nebulous will of the people of the United States. But I want you to know that I have complete personal confidence in you in doing it, and that whatever the outcome is, I shall back you to the fullest, insofar as your acts adhere strictly to legality. Under no circumstances will you be justified in taking the law into your own hands in any action not covered by the Articles of War. You will be the senior United States Army officer in a quarter of a million square miles of territory, because you rank both Lieutenant Ames at Fort Mojave and Lieutenant Golightly at Fort Yuma. What your relationship will be to any declared civil authority that Senator Bentinck may impose, must be left entirely in your hands to decide. Politicos have always been able to break the best of us—from Fitz John Porter to poor old Grant. That's the price of serving a republic. So however close you are forced to whittle it, *go by the book.* For if you do," Alshard smiled wanly, "we have a chance of saving you if it comes to court-martial—*and it damn well may!*"

"I think I understand you fully, sir."

Colonel Alshard removed his right glove slowly and he hold out his hand, "Good luck to you, Flint."

Cohill's eyes prickled slightly at the corners. It was the first time in all of their previous years of association that Alshard had ever used his first name. The military accolade, if you will, between senior and junior. Trust now—on the basis of friendship—a personal reaching out to break through the formality of the official barriers. The touch of a father-and-son relationship in the cold runway of the military scheme of procedure. "Thank you, sir."

With the Bay swept clear of fog, the *Amos Orr* across the wharf from the *Clan Cameron* was already casting off her lines as Colonel Alshard went down the *Clan's* gangplank. With her headsails bellying lazily in the off-shore breeze, the *Orr's* bow swung out slowly. Cohill walked toward the after gangplank of the *Clan* and stood against the rail with one elbow on it, a sense of deep loneliness full upon him.

For some unexplainable reason the memory of old Nathan Brittles, his first troop commander, came back to him down the long years in that moment. A snatch of his high, cracked voice, almost audible. "… reposing especial trust and faith, sir! Those words of an officer's commission commit him to do things that no amount of gold could ever compensate him for; and conversely, they mean he would *not* take all the gold in Christendom *not* to do them. An Army officer has no price, sir. That is his agreement in honor, as one gentleman with forty-five million anonymous American people who never heard of him—and probably never will!"

Old Captain Houget, his weather-coat turned high to his ears, took the quarterdeck a moment or two later, his voice trumpet crooked under his arm, standing spare and white against the evening sky. The duty quartermaster came aft and stood by the wheel. "Single up," Houget called. Then he bellowed forward for his headsails, and a moment later: "Cast off fore and aft!" Cohill reached into his pocket for his pipe. His gloved fingers crinkled paper. The Wells Fargo sight draft for his two thousand and fifty-seven dollars of back pay and allowances. He took the draft out, smoothed it, and in the fading light drew out his pocketbook to fold the draft away for safe-keeping. He checked the figure. The draft read for fifty-two thousand two hundred and fifty-seven dollars. His lips pursed at the thought of the completely paralyzed reaction of the clerk, when he discovered his mistake. In the excitement of the horse incident, he must have drawn the draft's face figure from an account column in the ledger adjacent to

Cohill's modest balance—and the man would sweat for months now in fear and trepidation until his mistake could be rectified. Then every nerve in Cohill's body pulled taut, for maybe it was not the clerk's mistake. *That's a lot of money. In one draft did you say, sir?* The money had been in his account and the books would show it just as the sight draft showed his acceptance of it. Bought and paid for, much more neatly than by a knife in the ribs. There could be no other explanation.

The *Clan* was swinging slowly out. Her tightened headsails took the sharp bite of the freshening wind and the ship stood sluggishly off on the tide on a slow beat toward the upper end of Alcatraz. As she turned stern to the head of Meigg's Wharf, a soft thump of air seemed to strike her and ease her on her way; then the full throat of the Presidio's retreat gun echoed across her to the opposite shore of the Bay in the wake of its explosive push to the still air. Looking back toward Fort Point, Cohill saw the colors ease down the staff slowly. In that moment, he also saw 'Theena. She was standing just within the after end of the starboard gangway with the light from her open cabin door full upon her, the wind in her skirts and hair, like a figure washed in sheet lightning, for she stepped into her cabin at once and the closing door smothered all light in the passage.

CHAPTER EIGHT

THERE WAS AN AFTERWASH OF LIGHT, broad across the western sky as the Bay darkened, and against it, Cohill could see the *Amos Orr,* ahead of the *Clan* on the port tack, coming about for a short beat toward the Sausalito shore before she reached for the Gate and the open ocean. Then close down to the water between her and the shore a light winked twice and went out, and the *Amos Orr* came up into the wind and all way bled off her. The *Clan Cameron* footed down fast and passed so close to the *Orr* that Cohill could see faces in lantern light at her rail and a man climbing her side ladder from a small boat below. Picking someone up after clearing the port. The irregularity of it was apparent, but the thought of illegality was the mate's as he stepped beside Cohill for a moment and watched. "*Amos Orr* could be fined a thousand dollars for that," Moxley said. "Who's that important to pick up?" With Alshard's last word to him on Inigo Barras, Cohill could have answered that if he had been a talking man. A movement on the quarterdeck above caught Cohill's eye, and looking up, he saw Senator Bentinck at the port rail with night glasses held to his eyes, watching the *Amos Orr* as her head came up into the wind again, her passenger aboard.

Then Bentinck saw Cohill, cased the glasses as if satisfied with what he had seen, and stood for a moment looking down at him. The wind brought his words clearly. "You have seen fit to set deadlines on this ship, Cohill. Keep to them. You nor none of your men will put foot beyond the limits you have established— or they will be fired upon," and as he said it a militia guard detachment under arms came up out of the after hatch and made shift to post deck sentries.

The *Clan* was taking the off-shore swell, rising in slow dignity to it, bowing deeply and running off heavily each time. The sough of waters on her hull played a steady overtone to the sea creak of her timbers. In the close-banked stalls, the unease of the animals settled to restless night quiet, the nitrous smell of them a physical gluten that slimed the men's faces and the backs of their hands. As a protective measure for the health of his men, Cohill set it up for one squad in rotation to be on deck at all times, breaking off by day and sleeping at night on the hatchhead.

After evening mess he gave his own six noncoms the ship routine orders, the fatigue details and the guard roster: Satterlee, Ohms, Fogas, Pumphrey, Clegg and the trumpeter one-striper Weigandt. Old Sergeant Satterlee wrote the orders laboriously in his notebook with a wet-sucked stubbed pencil. When he was finished, Cohill had them read back to him and plugged the one or two open holes Satterlee's slow brain had missed. "That's it then," Cohill said, and for a moment he let his eyes sweep the six hard-bitten faces. "Except that at all times all fatigues, including stables and all other formations, and break-offs, will be under arms. Light picket-duty issue. Hand guns. Twelve rounds per man." Satterlee and the three corporals met his eyes narrowly in question. Sergeant Ohms, his wiry shoulders hunched as he leaned against a pinion, raised his head in sharp reaction. Without changing his tone of voice, Cohill said, "and no man of this detachment will leave this area to go to any part of the ship except on my orders for stipulated duty. On such duty, no man will go alone. You will bunkie-up in twos from now on. Two men together—at all times."

Satterlee closed his notebook and stepping to unlock the chain of the improvised arms rack, began the handgun and ammunition issue to the men. Sergeant Ohms stiffened to duty stance.

"Second squad, Pumphrey—" Ohms ordered "—the deck tonight. Get your blankets and move up topside now. First squad—the guard detail. Marching on now. Fogas is corporal of the guard. Hatchhead here is the guard relief area. Lead out!" and he reached over to Satterlee and took his own duty belt and gun.

On deck again, after he had set up the second squad's sleeping area at the roped-off hatchhead, Cohill sat on the combing and went over the situation coldly. Not only was he decisively outnumbered aboard, but with the animal care necessary, his men would be eternally grind-stoned to fatigue duty in the cul-de-sac of the stall deck, with scant warning of trouble if it started with this uncontrolled mob aboard. As it had been on the deck when Lieutenant Haight was knifed, a personal hassle could flame to a free-for-all in a split second, and in the constricted space of the ship, his detachment caught off guard could be overborne by strength of numbers and snuffed out.

In that moment, he saw Captain Houget's spare figure silhouetted in the light of the suddenly opened door of the stern cabin. The captain had a cigar in hand. As if it were offensive to him, he turned it distastefully and looked at the lighted end. Then in an obvious gesture of disgust, he hurled it over the lee rail, slammed the door and stalked forward through the port gangway toward his own cabin. Acting from immediate necessity, Cohill crossed the deck to the gangway mouth and spoke to the captain.

"Who is it?" Houget peered with temporarily light-blinded eyes.

"Cohill."

"So?" with contained spleen and with no return of the greeting.

"I put it to you," Cohill said, "that this crowded ship can be dynamite. Your arrangements with Bentinck are your own. My detachment is aboard by right of government commandeer. I intend to exercise full freedom of movement necessary to the health of my men and animals. In the event of trouble, I want to know how you and the ship's company stand."

"Look, mister," Houget lashed the words out bitterly. "I'm a shipmaster with a clean ticket. I'm in this for my regular pay only. I don't take bribes. My owners made the charter to Bentinck, not me personally. And nobody buys me! What's bothering you—a gall-burn of conscience?"

"Explain that!" Cohill said sharply.

Houget snorted in contempt. "Explain? As the senator explained it to me just now? Would that explanation do?" He pointed a righteous finger aft toward the stern cabin. " 'Never mind Cohill, he's been bought for fifty thousand dollars—will he, nil he—and by now, Marshal Eudaley and Colonel Alshard at the Presidio know it by letter at safe hand, so anything he does or says can be completely discredited.' "

Captain Houget yanked open his cabin door, and the light of the oil lamp swaying slightly in its gimbals within flooded across Cohill's shocked face. "I was at Mobile Bay and the bombardment of Vicksburg, sir!" Houget cut the words at him. "I lost a son in Butcher Butler's Fort Fisher landing. I never thought regular Army shoulder straps were for sale in the open market, but I was obviously wrong! My back to you, sir—and keep of my course."

The door slammed contemptuously and left Cohill in the sudden darkness of the gangway's mouth, trembling violently under the accusation. From long habit, as he always had to do for his own protection, he beat the savagery back into himself so that he could think. But his thinking was not good, for the simple structure of his personal integrity as an officer had been cut ruthlessly from under him and he was momentarily lost without public acceptance of that integrity. It was of no earthly use to condemn the laws that allowed anyone to make a deposit in a man's bank account without his knowledge, for all that mattered now was the fact, and you cannot run to people with *he says he gave me fifty thousand dollars but I'm really an honest man!* Not when you carry a draft in your pocket that indicates plainly that you have accepted the money. *Time,* he told himself. *Take time.*

But in that moment, Cohill had no time left to take, for a slight movement flicked the corner of his eye, and turning his head, he saw Sergeant Ohms standing casually across the after hatchway behind him, thumbs hooked in belt, the light from below pooling his eyes in shadow. The following wind could not have failed to have funneled most of the conversation to him.

Cohill walked slowly out under the quarterdeck overhang. "What is it, Ohms?"

Ohms snapped his bootheels together, came to attention. "Just what the lieutenant sees, sir. The Lance Trumpeter Weigandt ain't no good for an officer's galloper. He's stripe-proud and fumble-brained. So I took the duty tonight, seein's you left the hatchhead area, sir."

"When I ask for a galloper I'll get a galloper, Ohms!"

"The 'tenant asked for one plain, sir, when he bunkied us up and issued twelve rounds and hand guns," Ohms said stolidly. "Don't need it asked no plainer with this setup we're on."

"You swallowed your guts, Ohms. You heard what Houget accused me of. Say it!"

Ohms veiled his eyes and pressed his lips tight shut; a killer, held nebulously to control by the blue shirt and the thin veneer of three buck stripes. Cohill had to nail him now and whichever way the sergeant broke could be high, low, jack and the game. "You're relieved, Ohms. Get back to the stall deck!"

Ohms nailed himself. "No, I ain't relieved," he said. "You need me, Cohill." His sullen eyes became cute-cruel. "I ain't relieved. I stay. For a half cut of fifty thousand dollars, I stay a long, long time!"

There was no break in Cohill's movement; it had no component parts. His right arm whipped like the strike of a coral snake. His hand flashed to Ohms' hand gun, snagged it from Ohms' holster, snapped it muzzle-up to his under jaw and cocked it.

He snorted short and hard through his teeth into Ohms' tight-drawn face. "Alright now, Ohms. I know your price."

Ohms' mouth fell open in astonishment. His eyes flicked to his gun in Cohill's hand. "I'm in arrest with what I know about this crooked deal?"

"To free-ride in the hatchway in shackles? Not a chance." Cohill shook his head. "To tell all the other men your stripes were cut for twenty-five thousand dollars? No, Ohms. You're *not* in arrest and you keep the stripes so you *can't* talk, for with the stripes nobody will believe that you aren't in this too, if you try to make them think I am!" Cohill whipped the gun's muzzle twice across the sergeant's shirt above his belt. Short angry whips, that tore a button off. Then he deliberately uncocked and turned Ohms' gun in his hand and, grabbing at Ohms' shirt, slammed the weapon back into Ohms' holster and dusted his gloved hands.

"Jeez!" Ohms gasped, and his mouth stayed open.

"And here's my back to you—for when you feel safe to plug me," and Cohill turned as if the sergeant no longer existed, and walked toward the forward hatch.

CHAPTER NINE

FOR THREE DAYS RUNNING, the wind held steadily out of a shade west of north and the *Clan* footing between seven and nine knots under full spread, ticked off Sur, Piedras and Concepcion and ran down the rain-misted Channel Islands past Santa Catalina and into the steaming breath of the Baja coast. And out of American waters. The platoon settled stolidly to duty routine, with no side pull. With lack of exercise, the high, nervous skitter of the animals simmered to dull apathy. They stood lifeless in the close stalls, waiting patiently for the eternal light watering that was necessary to calm them and the scant bran-mash survival feeding that was the only routine they could survive on without exercise. Sergeant Ohms stayed close to Cohill in most of the duties, watching every move he made with his small cruel eyes. But he worked well, biding his time, puzzling Cohill out in his twisted mind.

In that time, Cohill had sight of Athena distantly on several occasions, but not to speak. He faced the fact coldly that his vibrant attraction to her notwithstanding, he knew nothing about her except what she had been pleased to tell him. She was a stray under Bentinck's protection, proscribed from landing by federal authority and stained by gossip. He would give her no place in this duty he was on, even casualness which she might possibly be constrained to accept, and yet each time he saw her, the tide of desire rose again to stifle reason. Twice he saw the blackamoor Moktir in the gangway at her cabin door with a napkin-covered dish in hand, but sick or well, confined to her cabin or secluding herself voluntarily, it gave him no pause, for whatever was in his mind for her was held in rigid self-discipline.

Having locked Carracoe in to dry out, Cohill looked in on him at intervals with a pannikin of soup and found the man in the limbo of helplessness where the tide of drink ebbs from crazed arrogance to sick self-pity. "I was born Romany," Carracoe sobbed like a child. "Gypsy born and Gypsy it's written I'll die—*by the curse of the burned hands*," and he turned his face hopelessly to the wall.

Off Cabo Cabonet, Cohill found the cabin door splintered and the lock broken. Carracoe was on his feet stumbling around the filthy hole, half drunk again, his yellow irises glass-bright, the whites of his eyes smeared blood-red with broken capillaries. "I'm an old first sergeant!" he shouted in a bumble of slurred syllables. "Come up the hard way! Promoted to captain in action in 'lyss Grant's bloody burning corpse-stinkin' wilderness! Brevetted Major—and benzined out of the regulars in peacetime garrison after!" He lurched across the cluttered space to his peg-hanging blouse and tugged a bottle from the pocket. Shook it at Cohill. "To hell with you—and the stinkin' Army! And nobody owns the Colorado River country—except who can take it—and the millions in it waiting for the take—" and he necked up and drank long, leering at Cohill with crafty intentness. "And I'm going to have my share!"

Cohill watched him narrowly for a moment to separate in his own mind the blabber of drink from the surging impulse to truth that might make the man talk. For no one can ever tell absolutely in spite of the proverb. Not with drink, for it brings up the sting of all old failures, the lash of all old disappointments, and fuses them in the futile crucible of self-justification. Cohill had been leaning slightly toward the Gypsy with his own insistence to make him keep on talking. The rank sourness of the man's body and the stench of the fouled cabin rose into his nostrils and his stomach lurched. He held his breath, and then with diabolical instinct raised his gloved hands slowly toward Carracoe.

For a second the Gypsy stared in horror at Cohill's threatening hands, then he flung himself half-about in violent recoil from them, dropped to his knees and groveled trembling in the cabin's far corner. "*Don't touch me!*" he shrieked, his own hands held up, their backs to his tortured face, fending off Cohill's outstretched fingers. Cold fury blinded Cohill and disgust choked him. He stepped back from the wretch to keep from smashing a boot into him, and this time he left him to his bottle.

By late afternoon of the day they bore off to round Cape San Lucas the weather stiffened, with everyone on the crowded decks driven to their stifling quarters below to escape the drenching, deck-lashed gouts of water. Close-hauled, the chopped half-roll of the ship was deep and sluggish, with a thunderous heavy roar from her timbers every time she dipped her nose and fell off to starboard. On the stall deck, the horses were stiff-braced and screaming. The file-grate whine of the wind rasped across the canvas hatch screens like a continuous human wail of pain, and by full dark, the horses were braising against the stall timbers, rubbing their flanks raw. Sergeant Satterlee with the entire platoon was standing-to when Cohill went down the feeding alley on night inspection, rigging girth preventers to draw the mounts to the tailgates to brace on them, and lengthening and cross-rigging the halters.

The stallion was in a box stall on the halfdeck above the platoon horses, where he had traveled coming up from Mazatlán. Cohill had been up to look in on him several times, but with the weather stiffening, he made the box stall part of his regular rounds now, for he was fearful the stallion might break loose— and the second time, he found Athena standing to Turk's head, gentling him on voice.

Her sudden nearness in the half light of the passage lantern stole all his resolve. "How long have you been here?"

"Off and on since the storm started."

He stood silently at her side, studying the fine lines of her profile.

"Why didn't you get out of this mess in San Francisco?" he asked her angrily. "You had shore freedom. You could have gotten around the authorities eventually —you're an American by birth.

She turned slowly and faced him. "I could not get out of it. It was impossible."

"Because you didn't want to?"

"If you care to believe that," she nodded.

"Tell me why!"

"There is no reason why I should."

"There is," he said bluntly. "A woman like you has no part in a thing of this kind," he gestured aft and upward. "You didn't marry Bentinck—or did you? Before we sailed?"

"No."

"What then?"

"Don't force yourself into this," she said quietly, "for I cannot let you trespass upon my life. It is not tolerable that you should."

The words shocked him, for they were not a curt dismissal but spoken rather from deep necessity as if some explanation were due him. He watched her eyes closely, recalling the moment at the Alshard dinner when he had been so certain that he could have taken her in his arms, and again in the Presidio stable area, remembering her febrile panic when he had held her as the stallion's lashing heels tumbled them headlong together into the straw.

"My offer to help you at the Alshards'," he said slowly, "was as strong an impulse as I have ever had. I suppose that was trespassing upon your life. If it was, I have no apology, for you have not been out of my mind at any time since."

"That must not be!" and for a moment again there was the same shadow of panic in her eyes that had been there when she tore free of him in the straw. Almost as if she were whipping them right and left in a desperate search for an avenue of escape. As if she could run blindly now. To stop her, he gripped her wrist.

"Don't do this to me, Athena," he said hoarsely. "You know what it is that I am saying."

With her free hand, she pried at his fingers. "Yes, I know," she said, on an intake of breath, standing slender-tall before him, looking full into his eyes. "Let go of my wrist," she said quietly. When he let her go she turned half away from him, rubbing her wrist lightly, and stood for a moment looking off into the shadows, her lip caught between her teeth. "I told you that you are a very disturbing man. You knew that I found you so when we met on the road that first day. It is a man's instinct that these things are one-sided, but they are not, when there is honesty in them." She turned to him again. "You are a very decent man I believe," she said evenly, "so you must dismiss all thought of me, for I have not one tatter of self-respect to me to honor the good opinion of any man."

"Don't do that now!" he warned her sharply. "It's what you always do. On the one hand to present yourself for what you really are, and on the other, to tear yourself down like a house of cards."

"That is part of it," she said simply, "burned in habit in my mind."

"It is not a part of anything forthright—that anyone deliberately humiliate himself!"

"*Humiliate?*" and her voice rose almost to the pitch of shrill laughter. "I worshiped my husband! Adored him beyond all reason. There was a completeness between us that beggared all understanding. Every facet of me possessed and was possessed. I remained with him in voluntary custody all the weeks they held him prisoner at Guadalajara—" her words were tumbling over each other as if she had no power to stop them. "All the weeks that Bentinck's Neutrality Commission spent in negotiating the treaty with the Mexican Government. I know now that all of it was vicious self-seeking, but I didn't then. For his own ambitious reasons, Bentinck had to get Inigo Barras off—with safe-conduct to Tampa. To do this it had to be agreed with the Mexican authorities that ten of the Legion's officers be publicly executed in the plaza. By the names selected, it was obvious that Barras was making the selection to get rid of dissenting spirits and his enemies at the same time that he bought his own immunity." She looked steadily at Cohill for a second with a ravaged, haunted light deep in her smoldering eyes; then she shook her head once, fiercely as if to blot out memory, and drew in a rasping breath with her hand to her throat as if to ease the pain of it. "What I did, I did of my own volition—to save my husband. I will not have you think that the bargain was made to me. *I* made it to Barras and he agreed to save Paul's life. I stripped myself to Barras and kept my bargain in the shame of that filthy cell. I counted the first nine volleys. Then they fired the tenth and I knew Paul had died under it. It did not matter after that—that Barras laughed at me and left me to the commandante—the guard detail—" she wiped both hands to her face and shuddered in the helpless wrack of animal revulsion "—but that ended me as a woman—for as long as I shall ever live!"

There had been tense agitation when she started to tell the awful story, but it died under a great and simple pride as she finished.

For a moment Cohill had the shocked feeling of being a witness to something that he could not ever think about again. Of being shown it alone, for some worth, some integrity she recognized in him, and of being utterly unworthy of her trust. Then a savage surge of rage tore through him and his whole body trembled under the impact.

When he thought he could control his voice he said, "You have told me this for some reason beyond yourself. You did not have to tell me—" but in spite of himself his words broke into ragged hoarseness. "Why then did you!"

"Because there is a simple honesty in you that I will not have affronted. Now that you know, you may go your way without regret of me."

"I don't know, 'Theena," he said helplessly. "I cannot say what word another man would pass. *But I deny any man or woman the right to sit in judgment on you!*" and his voice was shaken with his intensity.

She half raised her hands as if to fend off terror. Her words were a throaty whisper. "For God's sake," she said, "don't offer me compassion. Don't give me kindness—pity!" He reached quickly and took her wrist again. "This way of your living that you find worthless to yourself—does it include Bentinck now?"

"I am not his mistress—if that's what you are asking me," she said. "Men like Rutherford Bentinck are contradictions. It is as if their natural deficiencies goaded them to dreams of power, until they live only in the potencies of their ambitions. Women to them are merely shields of pretense before the eyes of other men. I have used him wretchedly and shamelessly for my own ends. But it has not mattered, for when one lives in hatred, it strangles all pretense. It destroys all humanity, and when humanity is gone there is nothing left but the skeleton of existence. In Mexico I followed every faint trail to find Barras, but he had left the country. Half starving with poor old Oscar Willebrandt's debt-ridden circus in Mazatlán, I had definite word that he was in northern New Mexico Territory. That is the only reason I used Bentinck's kindness to come to San Francisco. I will kill Barras when our paths cross again."

"Yes," he nodded slightly, his eyes watching hers. "That would have to be the way of it—with a woman like you. But it will be in cold blood now, remember. Can you face up to that?"

"Face up to it!" her voice was acid. "I have lived for two grisly years with no waking thought beyond killing him!"

"They murdered Docher aboard this ship," Cohill said, "to cover for Barras' joining the expedition? To draw the marshal off his trail in San Francisco? Is he the man the *Amos Orr* picked up?"

For a second she stared at him again as if the thought was beyond belief. Then she said fervently, "That would be too easy, wouldn't it?"

He took her hand gently in his and his instinct for a moment was to bow over it in formality, for all of her innate dignity had come back to her and it was suddenly impossible for her to have laid her soul bare. Everything she had said to him was utterly unreal in that moment. "Athena," he said solemnly, "I have nowhere to take you but I will not let you go." Slowly she withdrew her hand from his, utter disbelief in her eyes. "But you must not say that," and her voice broke.

"I had to," he said softly, "for I would not give a continental for a man who had not been to the wheel and survived his point of breaking—nor for a woman. It's the battles we lose that count. It's the gay jackets we wear in pride to cover our wounds that make us worthy of them," and he drew her into his arms. She shuddered and turned her head from him. "I cannot—" she whispered "—yet."

CHAPTER TEN

THE BRUNT OF THAT CAPE SAN LUCAS STORM wove a diapason through the stall deck, to the counterpoint of animal throat-flobbering, the broken rhythm of stomping and frightened hoof-scrabbling to keep footing in the noisome, washing sludge. The parched cackle of men's voices up and down the feed alley was like grass fire, wind-whipped, with the chain shot of obscenity exploding viciously through it. The two hung lanterns fore and aft gave the stall deck the distortion of the nether reaches, shadow-shot and highlighted in grotesque detail beyond all reality. With the wind rising higher and the ship bucking it, the platoon settled doggedly to the long fight to save the animals, and the hours drained snail-slow across their weary minds.

Moxley the mate came down on an inspection tour. "We're beatin' up once again for San Lucas Cape on the third try," he shouted at Cohill, "but its no time of year for the Colorado!" and his Adam's apple twitched violently. "She runs a ship-killing tidal bore in spring, and the Golfo gets these sou'westers in narrow waters, so we'll be blown half-way to the top before she peters out, you mind!"

The men lashed on their own blankets as additional stall padding. Then their blouses. They stripped to their drawers in the close heat and bound on their sweat-sogged trousers and shirts. They cursed, begged, coaxed and prettied the beasts. There was no question of food until it was over, except for an acid black-coffee bucket from the galley, gone scum cold. The tortured hours of the fight crawled on endlessly, and men began to go out on their feet. They hooked their arms over the crossties in the feed alley and reflex held them, but you could talk to a man and not make sense and he couldn't hear you. Hours later you'd still be looking at his gaunt face, and he'd still be trying helplessly to understand.

Cohill was aware that he was himself sleeping on his feet, gone helplessly into the hard glass casing of waking sleep, with the core of his mind deadened but the fringe ends of his senses still partially conscious. Exhaustion rode him like the weakness of old age.

Seventy hours later he and Ohms climbed wearily up the forward hatch to the broad white light of early morning. The wind was torn ragged at the tail end of the long blow, with the afterbreath of the storm still scudding the *Clan* under reefed canvas, but the heart dying out of it. Half a dozen miles to starboard, they could make out the low blue haze of running shoreline. With unbroken land on that side, they were well up the Golfo, headed north toward the Colorado's mouth. The smothering Baja spring heat came down on the ship with the slow flush of body fever and drew her heavy stench up from below decks like the breath of a gangrenous wound.

The bilges were lethal with fermented nitrogen fumes from the animal drainage. With no cooking possible during the long blow, the ready meat lockers had spoiled green and the stench of putrefaction hung close to the crowded decks in nauseous skeins. With the perversity of the breed, when it was over, four of the platoon horses doubled down slowly in their stalls and died.

Working against the inertia of seasick apathy and hopeless overcrowding, Captain Houget and the ship's officers got the *Clan* wide open fore and aft—hatches, ports and gangways—to try to freshen her.

Cohill's platoon stumbled up on the well-deck and sprawled in utter exhaustion, the hot sun drying the tatters of their sludge-rotted trousers into hard, noisome encrustation. The sweat of their filthy bodies scaled to them in salt rime that hardened into tiny burning scabs of skin irritation.

From the cramped hours spent below in foul and stifling closeness, Bentinck's people crawled up to the open decks in slow-footed stupefaction. Five of them had died. They corded thick to the rails as if to get as near to clean air as they could, leaning on the bulwarks, packed shoulder to shoulder, the last men dropping to the deck planking and matting the waist of the ship from rail to rail with their exhausted bodies; unkempt, unfed and presently heat-seared into snarling, disorganized rebellion against all of it.

The ship's officers began to set up details of Bentinck's men at the pumps, but as soon as they were goaded forward to stand-to, they drifted away from the work, sat down and sprawled out flat. The Second Mate Olafsen was badly roughed and driven from the deck when he let his squarehead temper break over them. They gang-rushed him with the blind ferocity of baited animals. Houget ordered his mates to arm themselves, and the sight of the guns whipped the resentment to sullen fury.

By late afternoon the next day, stark necessity had brought a semblance of order into the ship, but the decks were still a shambles of weaving, restless men constricted to narrow space, with blankets and clothing drying out on lines and rotting food slops thick underfoot. Every time a man moved he touched someone and rage rasped sharp in the contact. The whole ship was short-fused to violence at the first overt break, and with the crew of the ship all repairing storm damage, Cohill realized that control would lie only in his own twenty-seven men and that blood would gutter thick if he was forced to exercise it.

The Gulf narrowed all that day, and when evening came, the mountains began their slow purple march down upon the strait waters. The spined mountains of Baja have no gentleness. There is a charred and ragged upthrust to them still from the day they were born in the agony of volcanic fury. They are mountains that are waiting, sleeping out the aeons restlessly, making themselves no part of the land, standing on the world's rough rim, tentative, aboriginal still, against the day the steaming waters will rise again. As Cohill watched them march slowly on the ship from both sides of the narrowing Gulf, he had a sudden consciousness beyond their gateway of the limitlessness of the whole vast Colorado country north to the Cañon Grande. Seven-hundred-odd miles of river opening up into it, with the wide reaches of land on both sides a huge segment of United States territory, uncontrolled, sparsely settled, unpacified, and dividing the whole southwestern sweep of the country from Texas to California as effectively as if it were still flooded deep by the vast and brackish sea that once had covered it. But a day would come, as he had seen it come in eighteen years to other parts of the frontier, when one small desperate battle would change it all, when roads and towns, schools and churches would begin to weave the fabric of civilization across that great, resounding spread of land. When twenty dead forgotten men would have forced the gates wide. In that moment he knew that some deep impulse beyond the individual must put a man's heart to soldiering, and that there was an unsung glory to the profession that never *could* be sung except in the hearts of men who had learned the elusive tune.

The day they raised Ship Rock, which was their landfall for the river's mouth, they sighted the *Amos Orr* at dawn for the first time since the storm. She was on the port tack off Sargent's Point heading to pass between Montague and Goree Islands. Captain Houget studied her long and doubtfully with his glass and kept the *Clan* on her own close reach for the point so that he would pass between Montague Island and the west shore. Then the *Orr* let a small boat down and it began to pull over toward the *Clan*. All blue was gone from the Gulf water now under the blood-red stain of the heavily silted Colorado. It was almost as if the water had thickened, changed substance to a consistency almost glutinous in the dank, flat bow wave. "Stinkin' Blood River once more," Corporal Fogas spat.

On the hatchhead, Sergeant Satterlee had a pair of glasses trained on Robinson's Landing. Presently he said, "There's an outfit in there under canvas." He looked around in puzzled question and handed the glasses to Cohill. "That's old camp number one from the survey days. What outfit would be down river this far into Mexico?" Cohill adjusted the glasses, saw the uneven rows of tents and a flagpole with blue colors limp at the top. The site was ragged and sprawled wide, with slight semblance of disciplined order, but it was obviously an attempt at military encampment. Four hundred men by the size and number of the tents, and in that moment a breath of wind bellied the blue flag and he saw the star pattern of Barras' Legion's Southern Cross ensign. He turned and put the glasses on the small boat approaching from the *Amos Orr*. In the stern sheets there was a gaunt figure in riding boots, staring intently toward the *Clan*, braced back against the boat's transom, not in ease but in tension, almost as if he would spring upright at any moment and stand to come alongside.

Outnumbered as he was and worn with fatigue, Cohill had one desperate moment of hesitation; then it became plain to him that there was only one possible way to keep control. That he must take it at the top, and hold it from the top down. He handed the glasses back to Satterlee and turned to survey the crowded deck between the hatchhead and Bentinck's quarters. With the open decks the only place tenable in the heat and ship-stench, the tension of Bentinck's people had relaxed during the night, but it was rising again now. It was beyond all word of mouth to control them, and every man in the platoon knew it. With no leadership, the weight of numbers would be beyond reason, once they broke full. One shout now, one overt movement and they'd overrun all semblance of order as they had on Meigg's Wharf. Brutalized men, half-fed men, packed like stockaded animals in the narrow waist of the ship, forced backward and jammed tight between the quarterdeck overhang and the stall-deck hatch, with only that open space and the sight of the ship's officers and the platoon's service revolvers to hold them.

The *Amos Orr*'s small boat came alongside and fended aft toward the starboard quarter of the ship. The crowd on deck surged to watch it, clearing a space on the port-side as they bunched together. The side ladder went down from the quarterdeck and the gaunt man in the boat below rose in the stern sheets, grasped the lower rungs and climbed slowly up. Bentinck was at the rail to meet him, and in the sudden silence of the watching crowd, he said, "Well, General Barras—we meet again!" and they shook hands formally. Then they turned and went below.

"Ohms," Cohill said, "I'm going aft. You're coming with me." Ohms turned slowly toward the restless, milling crowd on the deck behind that they would have to pass through, looked sideways at Cohill, and Cohill saw fear shadow the man's eyes.

"If you have a mind to even your money!" Cohill lashed at him.

In old Satterlee's face there was open, blank-eyed question. "You stand by, sergeant," Cohill told him, "and issue full belts fast. Fifty rounds hand gun—and unlock the carbine stands. Don't let yourself be rushed!" Then he sprang to the port bulwark and raced along it above the crowd toward the portside ladder, Ohms following, and climbed fast to the quarterdeck.

Moxley had the watch, but Captain Houget was still with him. "Get off the quarterdeck, mister!" Houget's cheekbones burned. Cohill took two steps up to the old man. "Anchor this ship!" he shouted into Houget's face. "At once, where she is!"

"Anchor? I'll—" Houget's hands came half up in an uncontrolled flutter and his whole face suffused deep crimson. His voice gurgled into a choking gasp. A muscle spasm caught his entire body and he pitched downward, his head striking the deck with the sound of a half-ripe melon. Cohill put his gun on Moxley's belt. "Anchor this ship, mister mate!" Moxley's eyes wavered just for a moment. "I'll anchor," he said, and he cupped his hands and shouted forward to Olafsen.

Cohill stepped across to the curved-top companion shield, opened the door and looked down into the black face of Ramillies Moktir halfway up the steps. He jumped into it with both booted feet, struck the man like a ram and carried his body under him to the gallery deck below. Moktir hit head and shoulders first, rolled limp on himself and lay sprawled with Cohill straddling him half-crouched. Ohms hit the deck right behind them, and his lips pulled tight across his teeth in a fiendish smirk, all fear burned out from his eyes under action.

"Holster your gun, Ohms," Cohill told him, and he holstered his own.

Bentinck's voice from the stern cabin shouted "Ram!" Cohill opened the door with a swift tug that crashed it back to the bulkhead. "Keep your hands on the table—both of you!" And he stepped into the cabin with Ohms a pace behind him.

Rutherford Bentinck was sitting at the upper end of the table with the remnants of his breakfast before him. Inigo Barras was on his right. Both men's hands were on the table, rigid in the act of pushing their chairs back to get up. Both their faces were turned to Cohill in indignant question. Neither man moved. A long-bodied man, Barras, his thin hair accenting the heavy dome of his forehead, which gave a grotesque narrowness to his face below the knobbed cheekbones while he held his head slightly forward and to one side as he watched Cohill with hot intensity in his deep-set eyes.

Bentinck wore a light linen jacket, a starched riding stock high to his neck. For a moment the question shadowed the senator's eyes still; then their bleached paleness frosted to cold fury. "This won't work, Cohill." He raised a hand to the other man. "This is General Barras." He moved his head imperceptibly. "There are upward of four hundred men of his Legion encamped at Robinson's Point waiting for my expedition to land. We are at present in the territorial waters of the Republic of Santa Cruz del Sur. By *de facto* right of occupation. It is no longer a part of Mexico. General Barras, as military governor, informs me that he has revoked the Treaty of Guadalupe Hidalgo. Therefore United States troops may no longer land here, nor pass up the Colorado River into United States territory. After my two ships are unloaded, you and your regulars will return to San Francisco——"

Inigo Barras cleared his throat. "Or be shot as insurgents. Now get out of this cabin," his voice rose in contained fury, "and don't come back unless you are sent for!"

Cohill studied Inigo Barras' eyes closely for a brief second. "Put me straight on one thing first," he said. "I am not allowed to land by this decision of yours, but the Colorado expedition is? It can land its people, unload supplies and use the Colorado as an avenue of entrance to the north? But the United States Army *can't?*"

"That is so," Bentinck nodded in studied formality, "by unilateral agreement between myself, as appointive Governor of Western New Mexico Territory, and General Barras. We are the authority, there being no recourse to higher, in the isolated position we find ourselves in."

Barras' shoulders moved slightly in an insolent shrug. "For twenty years the United States Army has not done one damned thing out here in this Colorado country, compared to the work I have done in the last six months! The Apache has never had faith in any previous negotiation—until I made my treaty with him—nor in the allocation of lands in the American southwest, until I gave him northern Sonora east of this Gulf, Chihuahua State to the River Conchos, and Coahuila. All of the territory my Legion was denied by the United States Neutrality Commission two years ago—*after conquering it.*" His voice trembled in fury. "But which it now, once more, controls — under my hand!"

"You're in conspiracy." Cohill bit the words sharply. "Long planned between you. You've played every filthy political trick in the deck to keep the United States out of this! How far will you run it out? To open treason? With the international line sketchily surveyed as it is, and the Arizona country in a state of all-out war with the Apache, your precious whole-cloth republic can creep steadily north up the Colorado into the whole of the southwestern territory, until one of you goes completely mad and declares himself emperor!"

Astoundingly, Bentinck's pale, bleached eyes never faltered under the indictment. He seemed to draw himself up slightly in his chair, as if the charge had subtly flattered his ego, as if he were secretly pleased deep within himself that someone else had found hidden virtue in him and had commended it. He nodded again in frigid formality. "If," he said, "complete political separation from the States becomes the only way to bring peace and order and sound government to a great and otherwise entirely wasted and isolated land—Where governments have failed in the past, strong men have been the only answer. I, sir, am such a man. Make no mistake as to that."

Dumbfounded at the bald-faced admission of what was patently not guilt to Bentinck, Cohill felt the compulsion of the man's eyes, so pale as to be almost deformity. Then the light faded out of them into a cold animal stare and he knew that the growing maggots of power-hunger had long since destroyed all possibility of reason in Bentinck, that the hot flame of his ego, fanned by the minor triumphs of his early life, had fused his madness into a solid threat.

"Come, Cohill," Bentinck said quietly, "you have nowhere on earth to go, and nowhere to go back to. In San Francisco, or Washington, you will be utterly discredited for taking a bribe. You've been paid your blood money in full to default—and that's on record. Now earn it. Go forward and disarm your men. Save twenty-seven lives for your own remnants of personal honor."

Strung tight in every muscle of his body, with the faces of both men washed crimson under the red film of outrage that suffused his own eyes, Cohill heard Sergeant Ohms' spurs tink slightly and he tightened his spine under the thought that in a split second more he would feel the spike of Ohms' gun muzzle in the muscles over a kidney. He had no doubt that the barbarism in Ohms would buy this bald-faced business and carve his own personal profit from it, and to hell with the oath and the uniform, but in that moment Ohms sucked in his breath and the words exploded from him, "Take 'em, lieutenant! The 'starditos!'"

Cohill stepped one pace right to uncover Ohms, reached for his own gun and leveled its long barrel on Bentinck as Ohms drew on Barras. Behind Ohms he saw the black man Moktir up on his feet, leaning against the door frame, his hands pressed tightly to both sides of his strained neck and shoulders, his eyes rolling white in pain. "For the sake of the book, Bentinck, I'm invoking the Sixtieth Article of War, which makes you subject to all other punitive Articles of War—as every soldier in my platoon is. You and all your people on this ship are, as of now, persons accompanying a component of the Armies of the United States outside United States territorial jurisdiction and in time of war. I, and my detachment, are no longer traveling with your expedition. You are traveling with me!"

He turned to Inigo Barras. "So are you—but in close arrest—until I can turn you over to the civil authorities on that Justice Department warrant. Put the 'general' in irons, Ohms!"

As he said it, the long hollow roar of the anchor chain racketed through the ship as it began to plummet out of the hawse holes forward. With the *Clan* slowly heading up to the swift flow of the river current, undercut by the outgoing tide, the sun ran its bright morning wash completely around the windows of the stern cabin until it now suddenly flooded through the open doorway to starboard.

Athena was standing on the deck just outside, as if she had been caught there in mid-stride. She held a gun half up and steady in hand, and every line of her body under the folds of her light, long-skirted dress was taut with vibrant intent. Behind her, the sun splintered in bright shards, flaming in her ash-gold hair, shadowing the drawn planes of her face.

Moktir leapt for her at the moment she fired into Barras. Her bullet struck the renegade from his chair, his face gray-slack in frantic terror as he turned to face her, doubled him over its arm and spun him in a ragged dance into the portside lockers. Moktir's rush for her, arms outstretched to stop her, bowled Cohill and Sergeant Ohms apart. Ohms twisted completely around, and clobbered the blackamoor to the deck with his gun barrel. Athena was in the cabin now in a crouching feline rush. Her second shot into Barras trenched the table crosswise in a shrapnel burst of oaken splinters that half-blinded Bentinck. Her feet skidded a heavy chair across Cohill's knees, and before he could grab her, she was around the table emptying her gun at Barras, firing down into him, the shots blurring their echoes.

When her gun snapped empty she fell back against the buffet, a bubbling scream caught so tightly in her throat that it would not tear free. The empty gun fell to the deck and she stood to her full height, her face a clenched mask of anguish. Then she flung herself toward the open door, the scream trailing behind her.

When Cohill caught her outside her cabin door, he restrained her brutally for a moment against her own hysteria. He got both of her wrists in his left hand, and with the right he began to lash her face front and back in sharp, buffeting slaps that jerked her head until the horrid sound in her throat stopped, and she stared up at him in wide-eyed pleading. "I'm free now," she gasped. "Free of it all!"

"I hope so, 'Theena!"

"I *killed* him—?"

"You cut him to ribbons."

At that moment, on deck the riot of Bentinck's people broke full from a reverberating clatter of booted feet on the forward well-deck to two muffled shots and then the thundering bull-throated roar of open violence. Still supporting the girl, Cohill moved to the head of the gangway and saw the murderous rush sweeping down on Sergeant Satterlee and his men, who were firing point-blank into it from the stall-deck hatchhead. At the after ladders, there was a crowd of shouting men, fighting to swarm up to the quarterdeck. Above all of it, on top of the afterhouse, the frenzied figure of Carracoe towered against the morning sky. He was naked to the waist, with his trousers rolled up from his bare feet. There was gore matted in the tangle of his chest hair and fresh red blood smearing the entire right side of his distorted face. His whole body was braced upward and back in a muscle arch to swing a great double-bitted axe. He cut it down fiendishly at a clawed hand reaching for him from the screaming mob below. The blade struck the forearm where it braced on the combing and the arm stub spun over the milling heads like a billet of stove wood, the fingers of the severed hand clutched in bloody benediction.

CHAPTER ELEVEN

COHILL REACHED FOR THE KNOB of Athena's cabin door and thrust the girl inside. Hugging the bulkhead, he inched forward again to the mouth of the gangway. Standing gun in hand, he was below and to the right of the starboard ladder up to the quarterdeck. It was choked with the rioters on the steps and climbing the rails, fighting each other claw and fist to get up to the visible locus of control of the ship in senseless revolt against all authority. Overhead he heard Moxley's whip-stringed voice trying to shout some semblance of restraint into them. He heard Moxley's gun fire and saw a man pitch down into the massed heads and shoulders below. At close range, Cohill squeezed off two spaced shots between the steps of the ladder, and the convulsive reflex of the men he hit tripped all of them halfway down the ladder's length. They fought there for a moment with the snarling ferocity of a pack ripping at its own wounded, then fell free of the steps in a thrashing tangle to the deck below.

With the ladder momentarily clear, Cohill ran up it to the quarterdeck. The port ladder was clogged with shouting men on the other side, and Sergeant Ohms, who had raced up the inboard companion from the stern cabin, was fanning his service revolver close into their faces. Moxley and Cohill fired across, and with both ladders momentarily cleared, all three of them braced to the forward rail, reloading.

Below, the whole well-deck was a maelstrom of uncontrolled violence. The mob had compressed itself so tightly in the waist of the ship that men were being forced up on top of the rails. At the stall-deck hatch, there was no sign of Satterlee or the men of the platoon. The rioters had the hatch torn wide, upending timbers and ramming them down into it. Then they began to haul the nested boats free and to drag one of them over the hatch to seal it. In the next moment they had the boat turned sideways off the open hatch and they were dragging it toward the port rail.

Between the two quarterdeck ladders and the surging mob forward, half a dozen inert bodies were sprawled like bundles of discarded rags on the deck, with the smoke from the galley stove cording thick and fanning low across them in the quiet early morning air. Outside the galley door, the man Carracoe had cut was doubling on himself, like a severed snake, trying to stern the jetting blood from the stump of his forearm.

A man in the port ratlines above the rail let go, arched over and struck the water spread-eagled with the crash of a splintered crate. It was almost as if that were some kind of a signal to the rest of them that there had been no purpose in any of it except a mad impulse to escape the putrid, close-packed ship. Amidships now, they laid onto all four of the small boats, dragging them to the rails. The one they had tried to seal the hatch with was half up over the port rail. Weight of numbers shouldering against its stern transom slid its keel over and it plunged down bow first into the water, submerging half its length.

As the current began to pass it astern of the *Clan,* twenty men leaped overside, thrashing in the water, clutching for hand holds on the gunwales. They pitched one boat down into another, splintering its bow strakes wide open. They trailed ropes overside and rolled side ladders down. They leaped free of the ship, they burned their hands blood-raw sliding down, they fought each other like cougars for places on the grablines.

In that moment, Cohill saw Carracoe in the doorway of the afterhouse, the bloody axe swinging in the Gypsy's great arms. As he surged out across the short run of deck, Cohill fired to a misfire and vaulting down over the ladder, spun under Carracoe's maniacal rush in an effort to trip him. For a second, as both of them sprawled on the deck so close that the man's fetid breath gagged him, he saw panic take the fury from the yellow eyes. Under its lash, Carracoe side-slithered, scrabbled to his knees and feet and dove back into the afterhouse.

Cohill hand-clicked the cylinder of his gun one chamber on from the misfire and stepped to the afterhouse. Adjusting his eyes to the darkness, he stepped cautiously into the empty passage with Ohms close behind him. Ohms pushed in half sideways to him, his body hunched in the narrow space, what light there was limning one side of his rough-stubbled jaw. There was a splintering crash and the leaping spectacle of Carracoe charging from the shadows, the swung axe biting full for them. Cohill's gun clicked to a second misfire, with the sound of the click lost in the crash of the axe haft on the revolver's fending upthrust barrel. The upper part of the axe handle crushed across Ohms' nose and forehead in a crimson spate of blood. The sergeant went down, pollarded, and Cohill, in the cramped space, kicked for the Gypsy's crotch. But as he kicked, his braced shoulders gave against piled coffee sacks behind him and the gun spun from his hand. There was dead silence for a long breath. Cohill got to his feet slowly. Sergeant Ohms lay on the deck, blood masking his crushed nose and lower face. Then, from the shadows Carracoe screamed *"The hands!"* doubled himself like a great cat and sprang again with the axe swinging. *"Cut off the burned hands!"*

Cohill came in close under the madman to get inside of the swing and took the swipe of the haft across his shoulder and elbow, his whole body exploding in the white light of agony. He spun frantically, tripping on coffee sacks, sprawling flat over them. The axe blade sliced down like a spill of molten silver and struck a hand's span from Cohill's right wrist. Coffee beans from the cut bag pelted into his face like hoof-spurned gravel. He rolled fast, jackknifing his knees, and scrambled to his feet. His left arm was out to the bulkhead wall to brace over Ohms. The axe blade flashed and he heard his own phlegm-torn warning to himself as the blade bit deep into the wall where his hand had rested a second before.

Carracoe lurched off balance, and in that moment Cohill tore the axe from him. He whipped it up and swung short and slantwise through Carracoe's shoulder at the base of the neck. The Gypsy spiraled off and went down in a blinding drench of gouting blood. Gutted of wind, Cohill stood stock-still, the dreadful feel of the axe blade on bone still grating in the haft to his hands and half up his forearms to his elbows. Then he flung the axe down the passageway.

He stooped for Ohms' limp body and dragged it backwards to the deck door, getting him out in the sunlight, the wreck of his crushed nose bubbling with his labored breathing.

Moxley was slumped to the quartermaster rail above them, his head down on his arms. The decks of the *Clan* were unbelievably empty of all life, and the echo of silence after the murderous tumult was like sound itself. One of the *Clan's* small boats was beaching on the shore about a mile below Robinson's Landing and the mat of rioters crowded in it were climbing out and up the soft slope of the bank, sinking in tidal sludge to the knees. Two other boats from the *Clan,* half submerged, were moving slowly in after it with men in the water around them, clinging to the gunwales, propelling them by kicking their legs. From the tent camp the shoreline was snaked with a long straggle of Barras' Legionnaires coming down toward them.

In the heavy cloak of his fatigue, Cohill leaned his head and arms to the rail trying desperately to fight down the impulse to laughter that curdled like bile in his throat. It struggled inside of him, and a knifing fear was on him suddenly that if it tore free it would take his reason with it. Drawn with exhaustion, he bit his teeth hard into his forearm on the rail, and a great sob wracked his whole body. But the self-inflicted pain of the bite steadied him, and through the taste of old body stench in his filthy shirt sleeve, there was the warm salt lave of his own blood where his teeth had gone deep into flesh.

Ohms' smashed face was pain-slacked under the dried blood and beard stubble. His nose was a swollen pouch of splintered bone, and his eyes were blackened deep to the undercheek, almost closed with the swelling. He spoke with agonized difficulty. "You could have let Carracoe kill me. Why din you? You had enough cause, sir."

"I don't know why I didn't. Somebody'll have to kill you someday."

"You'n me'll get along, lieutenant, until then." The man's broken face twisted into a painful grimace.

Satterlee's and Corporal Fogas' heads were peering up cautiously over the lip of the stall-deck hatch. "We got Dressler with a hole through the neck, and Oelrichs with a broken elbow, sir." Satterlee shook his head, still in a daze. "Where in hell did they all go?" Then he saw the beaching boats and his mouth stayed open in wonderment.

"Get a guard on the quarterdeck," Cohill told him, "and one forward by the anchor capstan. Make a ship search, Fogas, and haul everyone up on deck for a head count."

"We dropped into the hatch under them—" Satterlee was like an old man trying to explain the thing to himself still "and fired up on 'em."

Moxley was sitting on the top step of the quarterdeck port ladder, head in hands, his scalp laid open. There was caked blood in his hair and down the side of his face, and his eyes were not focusing. Captain Houget lay under a blanket on the transom top forward of the companion, still alive but lost to consciousness under the full impact of his stroke. His face and hair roots were mottled purple, and a monotonous whine bubbled deep in his throat in aimless protest at the burst brain vein that had dropped him.

"Moxley," Cohill nodded toward the helpless figure of Houget, "you're in command of this ship now, like it or not. I don't know what your responsibilities to your owners are, but I am going to transship my men and supplies to the river steamers as soon as possible and have done with the *Clan*. I will clear you on the legality of my position in writing, and I want certain transcripts from the ship's log. You'll take no further orders from anyone but me."

"I dunno," Moxley shook his head vaguely.

"You *do* know," Cohill said, "unless you want me to force you to the job. Put up a signal flag—or whatever you have to do to bring the river boats down here—to contact us and *not* the *Orr*." Cohill pointed upstream to the smoke of the two small steamers. They were feeling their way along, each towing an outsized barge, coming around the point in single file, hugging to the west shore to avoid the treacherous outspread of silt that shelves over from the east, and not fifty yards off the tent camp.

Moxley turned slowly around. "Them steamers are the *Gila*," he said, "and the *Cacopah*."

"Signal them down to us!"

Moxley stepped past Cohill and looked overside, studying the run of current and the outgoing tide. He pulled out a great silver turnip of a watch. "If the dropping tide will give 'em time," he said, and he cupped his hands to shout forward, his Adam's apple flobbering wildly.

Olafsen, the second mate, and his deck watch had been driven forward into the glory hole by the riot. They came out now doubtfully and straggled on deck. Olafsen bent two flags onto the mizzen signal halyards and swayed them up. Half a dozen minutes later there was a puff of white smoke from near the top of the tall funnel of the *Cacopah*, and a space after that, the distant bull roar of her whistle in acknowledgment.

In that moment Cohill saw Barras' boat from the *Amos Orr* come around the stern of the *Clan* on the current about fifty yards beyond her overhang. Senator Bentinck was standing with one hand to the tiller, the other thrust into his unbuttoned waistcoat. Moktir, his servant, was hunkered down beside him, his head bent to his knees.

There was the quality of a very bad painting in the scene, a second-rate artist's concept of a paltry moment in history—Bentinck's absurd dignity as he stood at the tiller, his head thrown back in arrogance. This small man, with his gigantic dreams of power gone beyond all rationality, was caught in the net of his own ego. Then Cohill saw that 'Theena was in the stern sheets, sitting in Bentinck's shadow; a small figure, her white cloak and hood against the merciless sun making her look even smaller. She sat with her hands clasped in her lap, her head looking straight at him, but with no recognition in her expression, as a woman does who sees a man for the first time, with no curiosity to see him again. All of Cohill's remembered tenderness toward her rose in a tide within him, blackened by an empty sense of despair. Then fury tore him at the reality of her there in the boat with Bentinck and he mocked himself for his softness.

He went down into the gangway, cupped his hands and shouted, "You're leaving this ship, Bentinck, without my leave—"

"Your leave be damned, sir!" Bentinck shouted back. "Make no mistake that I am still the appointive Governor of Western New Mexico Territory, with orders for federal military cooperation, and I will not tolerate a junior officer telling me what to do—no matter how big a gun he carries. I am the constituted civil authority and you will yet defer to me!"

"With four hundred armed renegades on shore and your entire expedition out of hand?" Cohill lashed it at Bentinck, "Even an ex-brigadier of volunteers—let alone a captain of Garibaldi's—should know better than that!"

The sting bit, and even at that distance Cohill could see the blood suffuse Bentinck's face. He stood rigid in a deep fury of speechlessness for a moment. Then he said, "I am going up the Colorado River in any manner I deem expedient to the interests of my mission. I have cooperated fully so far with"—he made a gesture toward the Robinson Point camp "—the authorities here on foreign soil. Ultimately this will be a matter for the Department of State. Whatever happens, you will be caught between, wearing only a first lieutenant's silver bar!"

Then Cohill's laughter burst from him and bubbled raw in his throat, for it is the eternal moral basis of all command that it entails full responsibility. If command is defied and deserted, its concommitant of responsibility loses all sharp definition. He was off the hook he had hung himself on. Deserted by the riotous panic of his men, Bentinck, in following them, had separated himself from all his supplies and equipment aboard the *Clan,* and by leaving them under Cohill's control, placed himself and his men completely in Cohill's hands. "You'll walk now," Cohill shouted, "if you want the Colorado! And when you get hungry enough, beg for food!" but his voice broke in a cackle that had no carrying power.

He was slowly realizing that his legal position was far from comfortable. Barras' death cut all tangible evidence of the conspiracy charge from under him, and the charge of treason lay only in Bentinck's verbal threat. Cohill was therefore acting under the palpable implication of conspiracy and treason, but without any overt act—yet—to prove it. The riot had broken *after* Cohill invoked the Sixtieth Article of War, and any court sitting on the case would therefore question the urgent necessity of Cohill's action. But he had no choice now but to go on with it, as he had laid it out.

As the boat drew off toward shore, Cohill turned away and stood for a moment looking at the door of 'Theena's cabin, knowing fully that the spleen that really galled him was against her. The door was open to the disorder within, and on an impulse he could not define, he stepped inside. He could almost hear her voice again, *I have lived so long in hatred that I have nothing left to honor the good opinion of any man.*

She came back to him then like the clutching hand of conscience, and he stood stark and sweating with her presence full upon him. In that moment he could not tolerate her aloneness, nor his, for the abysmal knowledge of the fundamental incompleteness of all men without women echoed in his soul, and the wisdom of primeval seeking was full upon him.

CHAPTER TWELVE

T HE TWO RIVER STEAMERS had rounded below the tent camp
and were headed toward the *Clan Cameron,* each with a flat
barge in tow, and in a few more minutes on the tide the tall funnel of the *Cacopah* was fanning acrid wood smoke across the
Clan not a hundred yards off to port, reversing her sternwheel
to warp in and tie up alongside. The *Gila,* astern of the *Cocapah,*
was coming down on the current to run under the ship's starboard side. On the quarterdeck above, Moxley was talking the
two steamers in on voice trumpet. Then he shouted forward to
Olafsen and the anchor capstan began to clank out scope, its
iron ratchet stopping the chain run at intervals with the tonk
of a badly founded bell. The anchor chain roaring free between
times eased the ship off on her hook, dropping her down stern-
to toward the tip of Montague Island. Both steamers had lines
aboard now, coming in close below.

Overside as the tide raced out, the swift flow of the blood-red
current of the river bobbled the ship as if great hands massaged
her sides, and a deep and distant thunder began to tremble in
the still air from the direction of the open Gulf, increasing in
its intensity on a rising scale, that was like the turbulence of a
vast fall of water from a cliff top as you move toward it. Each
minute it became heavier in its beat, and when Cohill climbed
up to the quarterdeck, he could see the great Colorado bore like
a squadron at full gallop returning from the Gulf to overwhelm
the lower river. Bentinck's boat, pulling toward the *Amos Orr,*
turned sharply about and headed in toward shore.

The bore was a burnished roll of steel-colored water in the flashing sunlight, dressed in a long, curving line extending from shore to shore below the two islands. It boiled bone-white along its majestic crest, the thickly plumed spray above it rainbowed brilliantly in the sunlight.

It happens only in two or three other parts of the world. The river's current, with momentum from half a continent north, channels swift in the lower reaches between narrow banks until it comes to head of tidewater at Heintzelmann's. Then the falling tide drops under it to the Gulf, and with a suck-out of thirty feet in some places, sluices furiously with scant pause of slack water to meet the incoming tide. In effect, the river plows *under* the tide, boiling the tidal return upward and over it and curling the bore forward into a broad wall of water forcing itself back up river in a roaring diapason that smothers all other sound.

Sergeant Ohms stood beside Cohill, watching with slow, bovine fascination. Neither man spoke, for the brutal majesty of the sight took all words from them.

Moxley, by letting out scope, had dropped the *Clan* close off the northwest point of Montague Island for his protection and the protection of the two small steamers with him. The onrushing bore divided itself into three parts when the breast of it was cut by the lower points of Montague and Goree Islands, like three separate troops at full gallop now, still holding line of front, but divided by the upthrust of the islands.

Then as the two easternmost waves spread wide to join again in drenching union across the upper flats of Goree, Olafsen, the second mate, shouted from the *Clan's* foc's'le head where he had his men at the capstan. His words were lost in the roar of waters, but his rigidly pointing arm was plain.

The *Amos Orr,* beating back toward Unwin Point from the east shore, was broadside on to the murderous waters, caught there almost stationary by the light winds. As long as men lived who saw it, the picture of that moment would come back to them when the crash of heavy water echoed in their ears. The *Orr,* still a part of sunlit life, was like an old animal, head up to sensed danger, muscles taut with the necessity to meet it, but with the heart-shot already fired and the bullet speeding.

In desperation the *Orr's* crew tried to turn bow on into the bore to head up to meet it. There was one dreadful moment of hesitation—a moment in which the ship seemed to shudder in all her limp canvas—then the underpush ahead of the wave thrust at her keel, and her port side rolled heavily down into it. The high bore wave cascaded over her and the rending shriek of her break-up began to racket across to them. The twigs of her topmasts snapped and brought her weatherstained canvas down on her in a gray shroud. Her keel struck down into the upper finger of the Goree flats and ruptured as she rolled half under. Lost in the rainbow corona of the bore, the thick, matted shards of her shattered hulk burst upwards like debris from a magazine explosion.

It was done so quickly that one moment there was a sea-strong ship and the next a shattered wreck. The bore in its relentless force was joined again by the left portion of its divided wave that passed forty yards west of the *Clan* and the two steamers and roared on up toward Robinson's Point. Stern-up in the insolently calm waters now, the *Amos Orr* was submerged forward to the stump of her fouled main mast, with an acre of cargo floating free about her as she sank, dotted with the heads and arms of her screaming people.

Aboard the *Clan Cameron* there was complete silence. Sergeant Satterlee with most of the platoon grouped about the stall deck stood watching the shambles open-mouthed. Forward on the foc's'le head, Olafsen's crew was braced against the capstan, staring. It was as if all power of voice had been taken from them. It was almost an obscenity presently when the river steamer crews shouted to launch skiffs to row up to the wreck for survivors.

Sergeant Ohms spat overside as a man spits over the show ring at a county fair in casual critical acceptance of what he has seen. Then he turned sideways and looked at Cohill, his battered face twisting again into a frightening contortion, as if in personal triumph.

Cohill went down the side ladder to the wide deck of the *Cacopah* and identified himself to Ormsby Godolphin, her pockmarked skipper. "One platoon you got, mister? Hell, Arizona's on fire, man!"

"You tell me about that."

"Ain't never been like it in all my time on government contract on the river. All the east bank ranches between Yuma and Mojave are gutted. Never before the 'Pache this far west—in force. Marauding, yes, but this time all the tribes."

Captain Ott of the *Gila* came aboard. "Like-a-this," he said. "The Upper Gila tribes drifted to Superstition Mountain in late October—for sign. Pinaleños, Chihuahuas, Coyoleros and Arivaipas. Maybe three—five hundred head all told. Must've got sign, for they cut in and began to raid the Colorado early November. Word was some white man was smoking 'em up to it with wide-open promises. Whatever—the Second Cavalry column out of Tucson didn't have a chance. On the lower Gila three troops ran into the whole kit and kaboodle for a finish fight and you ask me, the tribes are moving on south from the Gila. We seen talking-smoke to the east, all the way coming from Yuma to about forty mile above here."

Godolphin shook his head. "It's a pest-house at Yuma. You can smell flesh-rot two miles down-river. They got some Second Cavalry wounded in there from the Gila River fight. No surgeon and the Fort Yuma platoon lost half its strength in a running fight bringing them in. Like as not the 'Pache'll have Fort Yuma by the time we get back up. Crotch-knifed and burned out to rubble."

Cohill nodded toward shore. "Have you been in that tent camp at Robinson's?"

"Hell, no!" Godolphin spat. "We come straight down from Heintzelmann's this morning. That's Inigo Barras' old Southern Cross flag they're flying. No renegade rabble's writ in my contract. This is Mexico, and for my contract everything but a U.S. ship down here is *poison*. By the way, where's the captain?"

"Had an attack of some kind, heart possibly. Anyway he's unconscious and looks pretty bad. Moxley, the first mate, is in charge of the ship."

Godolphin shook his head. "Too bad, too bad."

"Well, what's your pleasure, lieutenant?" Ott squinted at him.

"I'll load you both," Cohill said, "until you tell me you've reached safety limits. Then I'll tell you when I want to start up."

With the platoon horses hauled up and lined out on picket ropes in the sunlight of the *Clan's* well-deck, Cohill and Satterlee went over them carefully. From the continuous slushage in the hold during the storm, their hoofs were softened and sensitive, but outside of the apathy from lack of exercise, the animals had weathered fairly well. By noon they had them swung overside to the barges, with canvas hoods to their heads, wet down against the heat.

Working on the supply transshipment, Moxley's crew had the platoon supplies pretty well started in off-loading to the steamers by the time the last of the horses were swung off to the barges. In spite of fatigue, both parties laid to on the work with the impetus to get quit of the job. All hands staggered noon mess, and in the full heat of the day kept doggedly to the work in hand.

In the late afternoon, the mate came to Cohill to tell him that Captain Houget had died. Cohill nodded. Something more to be taken care of later. Meanwhile, with his own ammunition and supplies in final process of transshipment, Cohill went down into the holds to make a survey of Bentinck's equipment. Under no circumstances could he take more than a part of it with him—but that part he intended to load against his entailed responsibility for the expedition under the Sixtieth Article and to obviate a possible charge of abandonment. He gave orders to the sling men to load food only, to leave all the expedition's tools, ordnance and hardware aboard the *Clan,* but to get the food started overside to the steamers as soon as the last of his own government supplies were brought out. Then, in the lantern light of the lower hold, he saw the stacked cases of artillery ammunition which Captain Oettinger had remarked on at the dock in San Francisco; in the neighborhood of three hundred rounds marked "Adaptable for the Mochfield Whitworth. Kittanning Arsenal 1865."

For a moment the criminal stupidity of the expedition's entire disorganization griped Cohill again, the hit-or-miss pack rat impulse that had prompted them to load blindly of any and all Army surplus made available to them by Bentinck's white card. Artillery ammunition —but no field guns! Then a cold prescience came upon him and he stood stock still under the impact for a moment, before he climbed slowly up to the quarterdeck and asked Moxley for the watch glasses. He walked aft and braced to the rail, adjusting the powerful glasses in the afternoon sun.

All day the men who had straggled down the west shore from the tent camp had been wading in and salvaging flotsam from the wreck of the *Orr.* They were broken into several dozen groups all along the foreshore still, with brush fires going, cooking and eating, and through the glasses the way they went at it indicated cut rations for a respectable time past.

The camp itself was almost deserted, and from where the ship swung on her anchor now, Cohill had a partial view up several of the raggedly aligned company streets. There was no wheeled transport anywhere, and what was obviously the commissary depot adjacent to the pack mule corral looked ridiculously scant for the number of men that had to be fed. Then it was that he saw the four-gun battery of field pieces, two of them placed on the foreshore of the narrows in front of the headquarters tent, by the flagpole with the limp blue bunting at its tip; the other two under canvas breech covers at the south end of camp. He had never in all of his eighteen years of service been in artillery action, but from his technical reading, he identified the guns as Whitworths with rifled tubes and he knew that properly served they could be as accurate as carbine fire on a garrison qualifying range. With no counter-battery potential of any kind himself, he and the ship and the steamers were sitting ducks.

By rough triangulation, he satisfied himself that where they lay now, they were beyond extreme range of the guns, but any move up river was impossible. To attempt to run the narrows opposite Robinson's through the fire of those guns would be suicide. Then, through the glasses, he saw crews moving toward the two guns at the south end of the camp. They took the covers off and began to manhandle the Whitworths out of camp, rolling them away from the sludged foreshore to the high bank and hauling them south to bring them into range.

Godolphin and Ott watched the maneuver through their own glasses. Moxley shook his head. Cohill studied the three captains closely in silence, for he knew that they would take no God-Almighty word from an Army officer with their ships in jeopardy. It took forty slow minutes to get the two pieces to the high ground above the beached boats, while they watched from the *Clan*.

In tight-lipped fury the river skippers cursed it out with Moxley. He could haul the *Clan* up and stand out into the open Gulf out of range, but not with the shallow draft steamers lashed to him. And neither Ott nor Godolphin would try to run for it now, up toward the other two guns at the narrows. "You damned fool," Godolphin shouted at Moxley, "with the *Orr* gone they won't sink us, to lose all the rest of the supplies! Stand steady here, man, and see what they do! It's all we can do."

Ott spat overside. "You know what they'll do. With us on the anvil and them with the hammer. They'll talk turkey now. Why not?" He looked sideways at Cohill. "Looks like your pants are down, lieutenant."

Cohill turned to Moxley. "The *Clan Cameron* is American registry," he said quietly. "Run up the colors." Moxley stared at him. "And ask for it?"

"You heard Captain Godolphin. They won't sink their own lunchbasket. Run up the colors!" But as the colors broke out above there was a compact crimson flash in the blue afternoon shore shadows, and a split second after it, that sound of fast rolling wagon wheels on snow that is a shell on its way. It screamed in high over the *Clan* and burst beyond her on the Montague mud flats. Before the burst echoed off across Goree and the far shore, the second gun flashed red and the second shell arched in short. A high spindle of water shot upward from its burst between ship and shore. Bracketed. A moment later, there was a white flag on shore and a small boat was pulling out, rowing toward the *Clan,* carrying the flag in its bow.

The four men went down from the *Clan* to the foredeck of *Cacopah* to meet the boat. Through the glasses, Cohill saw a man standing in the stern in a faded green tunic with ragged yellow epaulets at the shoulders. He let the boat come to within medium carbine range, then stopped it on Houget's voice trumpet. The man in the stern gave an order to his four oarsmen and turned the skiff broadside on to the current, cupping his hands. "Colonel O'Meara," he called through his cupped hands. "Chief of Staff to General Barras. Under a truce."

"I'll honor that status," Cohill shouted back.

"Permission to come aboard?"

"Come aboard," Cohill answered.

A tall, whiplash, blue-black Irishman, O'Meara, with golden flecks in his pale eyes. He smiled and held out his hand to Cohill. In spite of the remnants of his theatrical uniform, O'Meara had the look of a soldier and the eye of a good card player. He said,

"Cohill? That would be an Antrim name. Stubborn as the galloglasses —but not fools. Are you amenable to talk?"

"With Inigo Barras dead, who do you speak for, colonel? Senator Bentinck?"

"The Bentinck expedition has asked protection of my country," O'Meara said gravely. "I speak for the people of Santa Cruz del Sur," and there was the light of quiet cynical amusement deep in his eyes under the conscious solemnity he put to the words.

"If I don't parley with you the next round from your guns will strike into our waterline?"

"That would be the unfortunate way of it," O'Meara nodded pleasantly, "were we not to reach a friendly agreement."

"Talk, colonel."

"Aye." O'Meara drew a notebook from his tunic pocket. "We will not call these conditions the terms of a surrender," he said. "We will say rather that they are terms of agreement for a method of joint operation."

"Let me have them."

O'Meara nodded and commenced to read from his notes. "One: the steamers as at present loaded, will proceed up to Robinson's point and unload at the camp. Two: they will then shuttle back and forth to the ship until the *Clan* is completely unloaded. Three: the United States Army contingent now aboard the *Clan* will remain on her and leave the coastal waters of Santa Cruz in compliance with the revocation of the Treaty of Guadalupe Hidalgo. Four: safe conduct of the troops will be guaranteed by the Republic of Santa Cruz del Sur."

Cohill studied the golden flecked eyes. "The conditions," he said, "eliminate all bargaining on my side."

"That they do, sir, I'm afraid." O'Meara smiled. "For you have none," and he took a thin silver cigar case from the pocket of his jungle beaten tunic and offering it, murmured, "Courtesy of the wreck of the *Amos Orr*."

"But I do have a bargaining position," Cohill said. "I have three hundred and fifty rounds of Whitworth ammunition aboard the *Clan Cameron* that I can net up from the holds and drop overside before you can pass the order to your gang to hull these ships and force them to beach. Have you enough ammunition for your guns to stand that loss?"

Colonel O'Meara returned the cigar he had taken to the case and slipped the case slowly back into his pocket, his eyes on Cohill while he did it. "That I would not care to have you do," he said, "and if you were constrained to do it anyway, I would have you shot."

"Then," Cohill asked him, "you admit a bargaining position? How much time do I have to consider these terms? Steam is down in the boilers of both steamers and we are late in the day."

"That we are," O'Meara said thoughtfully. "What would reasonable time be to you?"

"You have fired on the colors of the United States, sir. An act of war. You have imposed the conditions. You state the time."

"Ah, you are a hard man, lieutenant." O'Meara's eyes twinkled. "But for a reasonable allocation of time to accept the full terms there must be a preliminary agreement. You are an *officier de carrière*—on the permanent list of your country's army?"

"I am," Cohill nodded.

"Then you will not be guilty of an official lie. You will give me your word of honor as a commissioned gentleman that you will not jettison the Whitworth ammunition?"

"I will. Against—" Cohill looked Colonel O'Meara's shabby uniform up and down and glanced toward the ragged groups on shore, "—your word, sir, that no attempt will be made to rush and board these ships, come darkness."

A very faint and mocking smile shadowed O'Meara's lips as he pointedly flicked at a spot on the skirts of his once gaudy tunic. "That agreement you have, sir," he said, "on the honor of an officer late of the Royal Iniskilling Fusiliers, which, I take it, will be more acceptable to your sensibilities than the Legion of Liberation?"

"It was you," Cohill said, "who brought up the question of official honor."

O'Meara bowed. "You will make your decision by reveille tomorrow. Affirmative will be the international code letter A at the *Clan Cameron's* yardarm. At first light, if we do not see it, we shall open fire." He looked at the three ship captains. "Good evening to you, gentlemen."

After O'Meara got into his boat and started back toward shore, Cohill stood silently for a long moment, watching the swift shadows of evening steal the afterglow. The mountains to the north stood out sharply against a broad wash of white sky for a brief space; bereft of a third dimension they were jagged black tin, sawtoothed across the river gateway until the full dark smothered them. Then he reached an arm to the side ladder and climbed in weariness slowly up to the deck of the *Clan*. For a long while he stood alone in the darkness of the rail, knowing exactly what he was going to do. But a feeling of apartness was on him and he could not reach into himself and find reality. He was not questioning his way of life in any sense, for that had all been laid out for him years before. That he had legal and explicit orders on a piece of paper folded in his pocket was as quietly compelling to him as a vision of the Holy Grail. But none of it had substance any more, for the presage of old age was upon him and he was heavy with the foretaste of death.

CHAPTER THIRTEEN

WITH MOXLEY AND THE TWO STEAMER CAPTAINS, Cohill laid it out. Moonset would give them ten minutes of full light after the start of the morning tidal bore again. Ten minutes of moonlight after the bore started to return again from the Golfo, and the darkness would be full. Once it passed the anchorage of the *Clan* and the two steamers, the flood would be with them. With the engines cracked wide, they should make the narrows' mouth in just under ten minutes. Starting right behind the bore wave, its roar should blanket out all engine sound, and by the time they entered the narrows it would be moon dark. On the chart, Cohill measured and drew his line where the steamers would be out of range of the two Whitworths that had fired on them from the shore above the beached boats.

"Four minutes to pull out of here and reach the line," Godolphin said, and he accepted the margin of chance with a curt nod and a gambler's phlegmatic eye. Moxley said no. Once the gun crews heard the steamer engines ashore, they'd open fire. To get the *Clan Cameron* away, let him go under sail and put Montague Island between him and the guns, and get away. Leave the steamers.

"You've got the clean end of the shovel all the way," Godolphin told him sharply, "but if you go first and leave us in the moonlight to those two shore guns, we're done."

Ott shook his head. "Against the tide, it'll take close on an hour to row a skiff to the narrows to spike the guns up there. In moonlight."

"Hug the mountain shadows. They'll be long on the river at that hour."

"O'Meara's no fool," Ott said. "That man is a fighting man, if ever. And if you fail to spike the guns at the narrows, we're blown out of the water going through."

"If you stay here, Captain Ott, how do you see the alternative?" Cohill asked him.

"To lose both steamers to them," Godolphin broke in, "and our government contracts to hell."

"A little more definite than that," Cohill's voice was steady. "I have asked for your cooperation in this." He looked at Moxley and Godolphin. "And I believe I have it now, two to one. Had I not gotten it at all I would have forced it, under my platoon's carbines, or destroyed all three ships as they lie here. Are you with me now, Captain Ott?"

"When you put it that way, what choice have I got?"

"Hobson's," Cohill said.

After the burial services for Captain Houget and Trooper Dressler, Cohill called his noncommissioned officers in and laid it out for them. He had rigged the spiking gear in the galley of the stern cabin, two flour bags emptied of all but the last five pounds in each with the necks of the bags twisted down tight to the flour. He said, "The spiking party will be three men. One for each gun of the two guns up at the narrows. One man to cover them at the boat. They will have an hour's start before the bore is due."

There was dead silence from the five noncoms. Then Satterlee said, "Lieutenant's pardon, who gets this detail?"

"You decide. I want two good men with me."

"Nossir," Satterlee shook his head emphatically. "It ain't gonna be the chance of us losing the only officer! That can't *be*."

Cohill looked at the five pairs of eyes on him.

"I take that as an admission of doubt on your part, Satterlee, that you can take over as second-in-command. You're wrong. You'll do very well, if you have to."

Ohms spat. "I go, sir."

"With that nose?"

"With that nose, sir." Ohms looked sideways at Corporal Clegg and Cohill recalled suddenly that Clegg had been at the winch when Boldoni was hanged. He nodded. "Ohms and Clegg it is. Bed down for sleep."

An hour and a quarter before tide-turn, the three of them readied the *Cacopah's* skiff. With soot from the steamer's fire room, they blackened their faces and hands. On shore, there were guttering fires at the gun positions opposite, and a sentry leaning on his piece in the firelight. They unbuckled their spurs and left them. They hooked up their hat brims fore and aft and crushed the crowns for irregular silhouette. Then, with oars muffled in greased rags, they started the long pull to the narrows against tide and current, taking their bearing from a jagged peak of hill to the northeast which would keep them to the mountain shadows that fingered long across the river under the dying moon.

Cohill counted time, for it was impossible to check it by watch. He counted steadily to the quarter hour, and found the skiff much nearer the steamers than it should have been. At the half hour, he still seemed far from half way. They bent their sweating backs to it, breathing broken sobs, with Ohms beating himself ragged under the pain of his nose. Then they began perceptibly to make in toward Robinson's, and at the three-quarter hour count, they were in the last three hundred yards, pulling close in under the high bank at the narrows to get as close to the guns, by dead reckoning now, as they could, to beach the skiff.

The count for time had been far too slow, for as they pushed onto shore the bleached moon was still ten minutes high to the mountains, and through the chill miasma of the river mists, they could hear the great Colorado bore beginning to thunder distantly from the Gulf. One other element dropped suddenly out of the bag. When the boat was beached, the bore wave, constricted in the narrows, would suck it up, splinter it and carry the wreck away in its rolling bowels. And it was impossible to pull it higher. For a moment, Cohill was rigid with disgust because that had not entered his mind, with all the rest of his detailed planning. He had taken the boat for granted to shove off in after the two steamers passed and the tide with them, then to follow on and be picked up on a beam from their bullseye lantern.

He dipped the two flour bags in the water and crawled to just under the lip of the bank, the black bullseye in hand, its hot tinny smell in his nostrils. He made his two winks back to tell Godolphin, Moxley and Ott that he was ashore. Then he smothered the candle inside.

"Why?" Ohms whispered.

"No boat," and he told them. With their rancid heads close to his own, he said, "After we spike, get out along the shore on foot and push on north to Howard's up river. Separately or together. The steamers refuel there. With luck you can reach them overland."

Then they began to crawl toward the guns. There were scattered guard lanterns deep in the camp and one at the headquarters tent. They heard a sentry's slow feet pacing his post in front and spotted him when the lantern light washed his head and shoulders. They counted his paces to twenty-five beyond the guns, and when he passed again, they inched slowly toward the two Whitworths. On the sentry's second passing of the guard lantern, Cohill crouched under the muzzle of number one gun and jammed the soggy flour sack down the rifling, forcing it home toward the breech to the full length of his arm.

He could see the great bore wave now splitting around Montague Island, its majestic crest flaming with diamond dust. Then he lost sight of it as the last of the moon wash died in the mists, but the roar of the wave was so heavy that it vibrated in the ground they hugged and they could no longer hear the sentry's feet. Then the guard relief broke in on the situation and they were pinned to the ground with the bore thundering up on the narrows, the steamers started—if they *had* started—and racketing along behind it—with only one gun plugged. Helplessly they waited while the relieved sentry charted his orders. Then the relief marched on. Cohill had been holding his breath to sharpen his ears, but there was no sound of steamer engines downstream above the thunder of the bore, no sound of firing from the other two guns, on the shore opposite the anchorage.

He saw Ohms' shadow crouch slowly upward under number two gun. Saw him ram his flour sack home—and they were crawling back to the bank.

The bore choked furiously into the narrows with the impact of a coal mine blast shuddering the ground. Spindrift shot up in a ragged white sheet forty feet above the bank top. The two steamers were so close behind the wave's aftersuck, that you could almost peg a stone to the foredeck of the one in the lead.

One minute there was roaring empty darkness and the next the dark-black silhouettes of the *Cacopah* and the *Gila*—with their stern-wheels lashing white water and their engines at maximum turn. Then, with the wave thunder gone beyond, you could hear the racketing engines.

Time counted down and cut as they watched the steamers enter the narrows. Hugged tight to the bank, it was like thrusting frantically at a door for it to burst wide—and having it stick. Then a sentry fired and bellowed in German for the corporal of the guard, and the whole river side of the camp came alive in shouts and running feet. Dark figures were racing toward number one gun and the first men to reach it barrel sighted it pointblank at the nearest steamer and yanked the lanyard. The projectile, with six inches to go, hit the flour sack plug and burst the gun in a splintered blaze of white light with fragments lashing the emplacement like shrapnel, cutting men down and riddling the ground in front.

There was a moment of indecision, broken only by the dreadful stomachic screaming of someone pollarded by the shattered gun. Both steamers were half through the narrows, almost hanging stationary there for a moment by the outwash of the tide from the flats and the bank. Then the Legionnaires must have decided that it was gun fault with number one, for someone pulled the second lanyard and the second gun blew white and lethal, both its carriage wheels scaling high from it and sideways like huge spinning pie plates.

Just before the second gun blew, Cohill lashed his arm viciously at Ohms and Clegg. "Get out of here! Separate!" and he saw their faces in the blinding flame of the shattered gun. With the light full in his eyes, something struck broad across his shoulders, his lungs sucked in nothing, and the light went black. When he came to, he was twisted sideways in the wet sludge just under the lip of the bank and it was still dark. The first thing he was conscious of was that the blow had been broad and heavy across him—not sharp. He drew in breath slowly and felt pain sear across his shoulders. He moved carefully to inventory, then his hand touched the shallow oaken cheek of the carriage with the trunnion plate on it. That had struck him coming down.

He rolled over and brought his eye level above the bank edge. In the light of guard lanterns he could see bodies lying adjacent to the blown out gun emplacements. He could hear musketry fire at the north end of the camp, a detachment up there firing still at the distant steamers.

Coming back down the sentry's post with another lantern, he saw Bentinck and O'Meara and two other men. Then he saw 'Theena's white face at a tent flap two tents to the left of headquarters.

"They got through, damn them!" Bentinck said heavily. "How soon can we start the column after them?"

In the wash of two lanterns, Cohill could see the girl's face quite plainly now. Bentinck passed her without speaking. He went into the headquarters tent with O'Meara following him and turned up a light inside. Then litter-bearers came through between the tent rows toward the bodies, and a patrol halted at the bank top, dividing to search the foreshore in both directions. A voice said, "They've got to be along the bank somewhere."

Still unhooked in his whole muscle system by the impact of the carriage cheek, Cohill lay where he was knowing that they would have him in another minute. That the patrol passed not six feet from his head and didn't spot him was unbelievable. Then he knew why. The nearest body lay just beyond. To them he was obviously a casualty of the burst guns. The litter-bearers loaded one man who was still alive and trudged off. Cohill rolled again in the fringe of light, drawing himself in among the dead.

He raised his head carefully and saw the body of the sentry sprawled on the shore side of his post. He crawled slowly again, flat to the ground. Inched his way toward the tents. The litter-bearers were coming back again. He lay inert for a moment, then, with the last of his strength, he rose and pushed through the flap of 'Theena's tent. "Cohill," he whispered softly, "for God's sake don't scream."

CHAPTER FOURTEEN

O N THE COT, Athena was half up on one elbow, the light of the turned-down lantern washing her hair gold. She stared at Cohill, crouched just inside her tent flap. He watched the shadow of surprise leave her eyes and saw quick acceptance take its place. She raised a finger to her lips to compel his silence, reached to the lantern and turned it out. For a moment the tent was pitch black. Through the darkness he could hear the faint rustle of her movement as she got up from the cot and crept toward him. Then her breathing was close to his ear. "You are all right? You are not hurt?"

He could smell her warm cleanliness against his own rancid body stench and the childhood need for female protection flooded back. For a moment he was lost in weakness, crouching there doubled upon himself. Then the lash of instinct cut back into his consciousness. He stood up slowly and the pain across his back and shoulders twisted him down again upon himself. They could see each other faintly now in the light of the headquarters' guard lantern diffused through the canvas. The twist went out of him at the glint of tears that misted her eyes. "You *are* hurt."

"I'm caught like a bagged coon," he whispered. "I have no right to compromise you. I'm going now, out under the back. I'll get as far from your tent as I can before they take me."

"No." She put both hands on his shoulders to hold him. "On the ship you said that you had no place to take me, but that you would not let me go. I will not let you go now."

They looked at each other, in silence that yet had sound in it—as of a bronze gong struck once, beyond their power to hear, but echoing in its reverberations until it was the fiber of both of them. There was no volition whatever, only the inability not to—as they reached out for each other. And it was as he knew it would be that night of the Alshard dinner, a throbbing, avid mutuality, that beggared understanding; a blending surge of instinct that needed no reason beyond the frantic seeking of their lips. "Hear me out," she whispered. "It was as you said it would be, in cold blood, when I killed Barras. I had lived so long in hatred that there was no humanity left. Afterwards there was no course except to go on as I had been. To leave the ship when Bentinck left."

"You think too much," his whisper was harsh in her ear, "you twist yourself in torture. Stop it!" and he held her silent again.

Presently he became conscious of one of her small clenched fists beating upon his shoulder; not beating to free herself, but beating in an agony of self-denial. She wiped her lips slowly from his, pressing her cheek tightly against his mouth. "Oh God, my darling," she whispered, and the light points deep in her eyes shifted frantically as they had in the shed just before that horrid spate of her laughter. "Forgive me my life—Guadalajara—and my love for poor dead Paul!"

There was an intolerable moment while she looked up at him in silence and he was aware of the deep inscrutability of all women, of the rages and pressures that rise and fall eternally in their souls, that no man may ever fully comprehend, so that in a very odd way suddenly it was as if he were not actually there. As sometimes happens in old houses one knows one has never been in before, there was only the seemingness of familiarity. Not the reality.

Then there was complete understanding and the wisdom of the gods was his for the moment. "Of Paul," he whispered, "I do not even want to know. But Guadalajara never happened because you still can't accept it. So I can take that from you. You can't even believe Guadalajara, so you had to kill Barras to give it reality."

"But you know that it happened?"

"Why certainly I know that it happened," and he held out the scarred horror of his healed hands. "Just as I know that this happened to me. The surgeon in Portland swore they had to come off at the elbows. Pouring chloroform with the bone saws laid out. So I dropped a gun on him and I'd've killed him if he'd rushed me. There'll be some mark of it on me all the rest of my life, but I'll live with hands and forget. Just as you will live with Guadalajara, and forget."

Then abruptly, there was no time left for them to live.

She pressed her hand to his mouth to stop his rising voice and her body stiffened at the sound of footsteps outside. "Adjutant, sir—you sent for me?" And Colonel O'Meara's pleasant Irish brogue two tents up the row in answer. "Parade the second battalion to move out north at first light. We will cross to the east bank at the same place we crossed in from Sonora and force the march on up river to Howard's in pursuit of the steamers. Pass the order, Mr. Petchekoff, that we will strike tents at once. The main body moves out one hour behind the second battalion."

Then Bentinck's heavier voice rode over it. "With ten miles to the point of crossing below Pelican Island you must put out a small flying column at once to push right through and catch the steamers while they are refueling."

"We'd better understand one thing thoroughly, senator," O'Meara again. "With General Barras dead, I am not going to run the risk of meeting the Apache in force until I'm positive of the worth of the agreements he made with the tribes. I won't divide my force in any way until we are all across the river with what supplies we have left and marching north on the Yuma Trail."

"That was not a suggestion I made," Bentinck said furiously. "It was an order I gave you! If you let those steamers get away, we will all starve to death."

"The steamers have no chance of getting away, sir. They must follow the bends of the river. Marching overland on the east bank, our mileage will be less than half of theirs. We will take them at Heintzelmann's, if not at Howard's."

Cohill was crouched at the tent flap again, gun in hand. O'Meara passed outside and a few seconds later a bugler sounded a call deep in the camp. By the texture of the darkness there was less than an hour left before first light He felt the girl beside him. She had been dressing while he crouched there and she finished buttoning her blouse. "We have a chance," she said. "With work parties in the streets and the darkness," and there was quiet conviction in her whisper.

"Are you ready?"

They lay flat on the ground at the rear of the tent and Cohill reached under and pulled up two of the wall pegs. They crawled out into the cold morning darkness and lay listening. Deep in the camp there was the cross-laced trill of noncoms' whistles, and the mules picked it up, horning the mists in rusty-throated protest.

They got to their feet and started to walk slowly toward the north end of the alley between the back walls of the first two rows of tents. Men were turning to inside both rows, cursing the move-out, stumbling toward the latrines. The camp smell of dung and of old sweat and damp canvas skeined through the stale smoke that hung in the still air.

Masked by the last tent in the row, they stopped at the sound of closeby footsteps. There was open space beyond and a section was marching diagonally across it coming up from the direction of the commissary area. Not ten feet from them, the noncom halted it in German-burred English, called off a squad to go down to load headquarters baggage, and set the other two squads to strike canvas in the first two tent rows. As the section broke ranks and straggled into the two streets, Cohill and the girl stepped out of the alley between and started across the open space, so close to the men that they could smell them.

Close in to their left now a large detachment was drawn up for reveille roll call and the names were batting the air like laths struck to baled cotton, a rolling flat monotone of syllables with the crack of *"Here"* punctuating the sounds. Then suddenly they were walking right through a group of six men coming in toward them out of the darkness, straggling out of formation. The moment of passing by them was intolerable. Breathholding— with armpit sweat breaking cold and watery thin. Then the footsteps were behind them and they were at the north edge of camp, going down the gradual slope from the higher ground of the point toward the river's edge. They began to jogtrot, with shoulder pain riding Cohill like an iron-spurred jockey, but with time the only club they had to grab for.

There were white mists walled high over the tidal flats across river to the eastward, where the cool night breath of the Sonora Desert meets the warm flow of the Colorado. Mists that were crenelated ramparts, walling the night off on that side like towering masonry. Then the dawn began to fray the tops into tattered gonfalons, and with the sun coming up over the parched sands, the mists flamed crimson as if fire were set at the base to gut them, and in five minutes they were gone with the whole spread of the heating desert lying to the eastward with distant mesas beyond, their flat tops flaming gold.

Ohms' low call stopped them suddenly. "Sweet whoosis, *lieutenant!*" and the sergeant and Corporal Clegg were standing bankside, like two black-faced scarecrows against the morning. "We was waiting—and hoping," Clegg said. "Can't neither of us swim. 'Morning, lady," Ohms bobbed his head.

They put themselves to a hundred paces running and a hundred walking with the sweat soaking thick under the rise of heat and no words possible in the lung rasp that seared their chests. With the night river-damp still holding the surface of the ground, they pushed on hard against the first hour of the rising sun, in the safety of raising no telltale dust until then. But in that hour the knowledge was compulsive that they had a whole battalion on the march behind them, and from the last, low rise before the river bends west, they could see the column only a few miles distant, beginning to raise its own dust.

Where the river bends, they were opposite the end of Pelican Island and the broad silt flats that tongue out from the eastern shore. Ahead they saw a brush road corduroyed from the bank lip to the water's edge, with Seri Indian balsas, like great reed baskets, drawn up along the foreshore. The crossing point to the east bank.

They pushed down to it and, to delay the pursuit, Cohill and the two noncoms began to launch the balsas, shoving them out into the blood-red current of the Colorado. When they were all afloat, they got into the smallest and started to paddle across river. It took a good half-hour to fight the current and reach the opposite bank. They waded out through a rattling mat of blue crabs and climbed the bank. The fast-rising heat had the air thinly festered with flesh rot, and buzzards rose below them in ragged clouds. The bodies from the wreck of the *Amos Orr*. For almost a mile, the tide had matted them across the end of the flats, as if with an orderly instinct to keep the dead together.

Still well below the crossing, the sun was flashing silver on the rifles of O'Meara's second battalion march column. Its dust banner flagged up high behind it, its head in the clear air, knocking it off at a fast route step in spite of the heat. They were battle-conditioned mercenaries, steady to the road and jungle hard, in hot pursuit of the vital steamers. Then the troops saw the twenty balsas floating toward them and the column halted at once and sent detachments to the bank to swim out and retrieve them.

With six miles still to go up the east bank to get to Howard's, Cohill set their pace against his own lash of pain and led off up through the fringing Bermuda grass to the flat ground, which was a solid trace, ribbed above the river on eroded buttresses of decomposed sandstone. With 'Theena behind him and Ohms and Clegg in the rear, they toiled up the rise until the shoulder of Pelican Island was behind them and they could see the tiny dock and shed distantly at Howard's. The steamers were not there.

"Gave us up for gone." Ohms sat down disconsolately and wiped his bleeding nose on his filthy sleeve. The girl looked at Cohill. He shook his head. "From the map," he said, "it's thirteen more miles overland to Heintzelmann's. We have no second choice."

They started out again, moving stiffly and slowly under the murderous sun, plodding on toward Howard's. Then Corporal Clegg shouted suddenly and pointed toward the sun-cindered hogback between the creek that comes in opposite Pelican Island and the broad sweep east again that the Colorado makes beyond the Island. There was a line of horsemen leading their mounts up the rise on foot, crawling like ants up the near shoulder, single file, spaced out. For one awful moment of doubt they stared under their shading hands, then it was unmistakably Satterlee with the platoon. They could see the black, raked hats and the faded blue.

Cohill pushed at Ohms and Clegg to stand out on his right. He touched the girl's shoulder to stand her out left to make four clear figures in line of front. Then he drew his hand gun and emptied it in six spaced shots into the oven-baked air.

For a moment the horse column kept right on leading up the rise three miles distant from them. Then it halted, straggling in on itself from the rear. Up at its head, the sun glinted in two ice splinters on the lenses of field glasses, searching toward them to identify the source of the shots.

CHAPTER FIFTEEN

WEIGANDT AND GILHOOLIE HAD BEEN KILLED by small-arms fire as the steamers navigated the narrows. Corporal Fogas had a smashed left forearm. The duty strength of the platoon now was one officer and twenty-two men, with Fogas and Oelrichs light duty from wounds—riding the *Cacopah*.

At Howard's, Sergeant Satterlee had disembarked the horse herd to condition it, and he had put the platoon to leading the animals overland the thirteen miles upstream to Heintzelmann's where he would meet the steamers again. Faced with the overwhelming fact of command, the old man had scuttled back into the safety of the book, completely incapable of any thinking beyond the routine of his thirty years' horse service. But he had all the mounts with him, including the stallion. And he had done the right thing.

"Sure glad. God bless you, lieutenant!"

From the hog back there was enough elevation for a clear view back on both sides of the river. Cohill made a careful glass reconnaissance. The Legion's second battalion was halted on the west bank at the crossing place, and two balsas of men were in midstream, paddling for the east bank. They had retrieved all but one of the other balsas. The main column, with pack mules, was cording the dust thick not three miles below the crossing. But he could not spot the two Whitworth guns that were left to O'Meara. Instinctively he knew why. The *Clan Cameron* had gotten clean away to the Gulf when the steamers left her, carrying the vital ammunition, and without it, the guns were worthless. So they had been left.

It was ten minutes to eleven o'clock, with three and a half horse-walking march hours ahead of the platoon to get to Heintzelmann's. Cohill estimated that in that three and a half hours, the entire Legion would be across on the east bank, and at the disciplined march pace he had observed, eight miles on the way north; that is to say, two miles north of Howard's with only eleven miles ahead of them to reach Heintzelmann's. With those eleven miles still facing O'Meara, his column would have knocked off sixteen miles already that day. But with the necessity upon them to take the steamers at all costs, he could push a flying column ahead of the main body and reach Heintzelmann's by nightfall.

Cohill's intolerable position came full home to him. In a foreign country still, until he reached the doubtful handicapped sanctuary of Fort Yuma, he had a gaunt and hostile army in close pursuit behind him with no alternative if they were to survive but to destroy him and seize the steamers. And every mile he moved north, he came a mile closer to the helpless Yuma garrison and the hostile Apache concentration somewhere in the hills along the eastern flow of the river.

Cohill gave the glasses back to Satterlee. He made a thorough hoof inspection and mounted the platoon at the walk for an hour with the noon heat rising like a furnace breath from the earth. He watered upstream of a fresh creek, rested and pushed on. He led his column into Heintzelmann's about four o'clock, where the *Gila* and the *Cacopah* were tied up waiting for him, and went aboard the *Cacopah* at once for a conference with the two captains, Ott and Godolphin.

They spread the explorations and surveys map—lieutenant Joseph Yves' 1858 relief—on the cubby-locker top, with the indicated new channels the Colorado had made for itself since. By the corkscrewing of the river, there were forty-six steamer miles to run up to reach Ogden's Landing, the next fueling point above Heintzelmann's. With the barges in tow and against the current,

Godolphin estimated a minimum time of fifteen hours for the passage, one mile slower in each hour than normal infantry march time. By the same token, the march route overland traced out only twenty-six miles to Ogden's.

Timed and spaced it came out this way. If the steamers started upstream now, they could not possibly reach Ogden's before eleven o'clock the next morning. Even if they did, the Legion starting at dawn from Heintzelmann's could march over-land to Ogden's in six hours—and be only an hour behind them. If the steamers grounded in darkness—that hour would be gone so fast that a quick shot wouldn't nick it.

They loaded the horses and shoved off, and in an hour dark-ness came down and there was no light but the blood-red glow of the fire doors on the red flow of the river until the moon broke over the mountains at about half-past ten. By lantern, Cohill still studied the map, but it came out no other way. On the frontier, there is no course of life that lends to wishful thinking. Life rests only on what the enemy *can* do, not on what you hope he will do. Guess, hope or wish and your bones bleach white.

Cohill folded the map and stepped out beside Godolphin at the *Cacopah*'s wheel. The consciousness was full upon him that he had nothing left to draw on. He was drained to the raw fiber of mere existence by the past two years on the Columbia Survey, and his margin of resilience was cut to zero by the ordeal since San Francisco. It occurred to him that he was done, and for a moment there was no will left in him even to resist the thought. He breathed deeply against the impulse of a reflex sob and the bitterness of defeat was in his nostrils.

Godolphin, standing at his great wheel, feeling the channel ahead by memory, spoke to him sideways. "It's a few miles north of here to the east that Ott and I saw the last spindles of talking smoke, when we came downstream. We saw it all the way down here, off and on, from below Yuma," he jerked his head to the right bank. "You ask me, the tribes moved after the Gila River fight with the Second Cavalry and they are in there somewhere still—camped to the high ground. Within easy reach of the river for water."

Cohill had no words for answer. He turned and looked off into the darkness toward the shore. Then through the apathy of his deep exhaustion, the memory came sharply back to him of O'Meara's answer to Bentinck outside the tent. Whatever agreements Inigo Barras had made with the tribes the Irishman was not too confident of them. It was Cohill's own long experience that it is one thing to make a treaty with the barbarian but quite another to continue it long without continued payments. The interest on whatever down payment Barras had made was the defeat of the Second Cavalry on the Gila, but the lands Barras had promised south in Mexico were still remote to this tribal movement, and nebulous, for the Apache habit of mind does not define the future too clearly. It was quite plausible that Barras might have planned to meet the tribes down here again, but if that were so, with Barras dead, the headman would be suspicious of new faces, for white soldiers were white soldiers and had been since the Spaniard.

At that moment, the long chance came alive in Cohill's mind like the white echo of the two burst Whitworths, but it ceased at once to be long, for it was the only chance possible. He went back to the map and made another careful survey. Then he stepped to the cubby door and looked down at 'Theena. She was sleeping peacefully with the moonwash on the finely boned planes of her face.

A very strange thing happened then to Cohill. He became suddenly aware of the inexorable progression of all life—before and beyond the individual. At once, he was a little boy at his father's booted knee, and at the same time he was staring down in wonderment at a child's face at his own knee, touching the crisp boyish hair and looking into the face of his own son, still blurred beyond the mists of time. The thunder of reality reverberated back across his mind then until he was trembling slightly in the backs of his knees. He drew in breath deeply and walked slowly forward, to Godolphin at the wheel. "To be absolutely sure of getting your wood-fuel aboard at Ogden's, I will disembark my platoon again about an hour after sunrise. We'll skirmish south along the Yuma Trail, feeling for the Legion's advance guard. When we find it, we'll delay their march—if that becomes necessary."

He had to say the words carefully, for his gaunt face muscles were clenched tight now and they drew at his lips. He was twitching violently when he rolled in his blanket. His eyes stung and his heart raced, and a gloating fury took his whole body. Then eventually he slept.

Before the sun was up to burn the mists, the steamers tied up bankside and the platoon led the mounts off and saddled up at a point about eight overland miles below Ogden's Landing. The steamers shoved off again at once, continuing on their laboring way upstream.

At the walk, the platoon led straight east for two miles and found no trace of the Legion's march. They turned south and rode several slow miles before they saw the march column's dust, far enough back still for a fair time cushion. Cohill turned north again then and dismounted once more, led his men slowly toward Ogden's Landing with a three-man point well ahead of him, and a flank guard thrown out to the east. At nine o'clock they saw a smoke spindle rising high and broken with talk and saw the answer from the eastern hills.

It was half-past ten when the platoon trotted into Ogden's. John Ogden was dead, with the trail of his empty brass leading from his burned shack to the steamer dock. His wife's body lay beside him, with his own mercy shot through her head. Both of them left in honor—unmutilated—for his bravery. But the two Zuñi woodcutters were staked out, dead of the slow fires, fly-gutted, netted black against the sun. There were the marks of about thirty ponies.

Sergeant Ohms dismounted and picked up dung, shredding it between his hands. He sifted it through his fingers and held out a spread of half-digested oat husks. "Second Cavalry oats— you bet your knocks," he grunted. "Show me an oat patch in all Arizona that the Apaches plant themselves."

With an outguard pushed north a thousand yards up the Yuma trail, Cohill sent Pumphrey's squad off south again toward the Legion's line of march. They buried the Ogden people and watered the horses. Then they found the Pinaleño. He was burrowed in mud in the Bermuda grass by the water's edge and Foley kicked the knife from his hand before he could leap and gut with it. Hauled out, they found his shin shattered by a .44 and the bone ridge above his left eye carried away in an inch-and-a-half long gouge. The membrane palpitated below it when he breathed. Knocked out by it, and unseen, he had been left by inadvertence, for the Apache always takes his wounded out and buries his dead in obliterated graves.

The hatred in the obsidian eyes flamed up into Cohill's as he stood over him. The man answered nothing by sign or sound to Cohill's stilted questioning.

"You want I should make him talk, sir?" Ohms snarled. "I got good methods. I been garrisoned on Blood River before." Ohms waded down the bank and scanned the waters closely. Then, from John Ogden's beached skiff, he rigged a hook and cast the length of line in. A few minutes later he had his fish. The Pinaleño screamed like a hill cat when Ohms held it close to his mouth. "Talk you stinking *hoor!*" Ohms shouted at him, "or I'll stuff this down your gullet! Gila Apaches go to specialized perdition if they eat fish. Ask him what you want, lieutenant. He'll tell you now!"

Cohill had the Pinaleño propped up, and started to try to draw it out of him with sketchy words and with a stick in the dirt while Ohms held the fish close. The Apache trembled as if violent after-fever chill had him. But he talked. He never took his eyes from the fish. Slowly, in abysmal horror, he answered. The tribes were a dozen miles east on the high ground, where Godolphin thought they might be. They were strung out in separate camps, maybe two hundred Apaches, maybe five hundred in all. You can never tell, for the Apache is essentially an individualist. He has no concept of numbers over the ten of his fingers. He never thinks in terms of numbers, except in the minimum sense of what he feels necessary for his attack. He seldom overestimates that necessity, and when he does, he feels a degrading loss of face, for race memory is long in his heritage, and it may well reach back to Ghengis Khan.

When Cohill was finished, Ohms made a sudden thrust of arm and forced the head of the fish into the Apache's mouth. With his knee smashed upward to the chin, he snapped the hostile's jaw closed on it and slapped the headless fish across the tortured rigid face, streaking it with blood. For one ghastly moment the black eyes implored. Then the savage stiffened the muscles in his entire body, convulsed his throat until the cords quivered, and he died, with the fishhead in his mouth, almost by the wall to die. By one scabrous ankle, Ohms hurled his body into the Colorado.

The cards were falling so close into place that there was a nerve quiver trembling through the drag of Cohill's anxiety. Eating mechanically, his throat went bone dry and he vomited with stomach reflex. As he straightened up, he heard the distant staccato of scattered carbine fire from Pumphrey's squad to the south, lost at once in the deep guttural of musketry. Ten minutes later the bow of the *Cacopah* rounded the river bend below.

By the time the *Gila* was tied up, with her main bearing smoking under dousing pails of river water, Pumphrey's squad had galloped back in from the trail south with word that the advance guard of the Legion was just under five miles south of Ogden's, pushing hard.

With all hands turned to, they loaded all the cut wood aboard, larded down the *Gila's* worn bearing and got both steamers on their way, just as the Legion's skirmish line came over the low southern ridge and opened fire at extreme range.

Cohill led out on the bridle, deliberately, walking his command along the swampy fringe that cuts in between the landing and the trail, and mounting only after he reached the trail. Drawing north at the trot then, he ran out five fast miles to put another hour between him and the Legion. Then, with four hours left of daylight, he watered and filled canteens and skirted off the trail heading slowly across the desert toward the lower rim of hills to the east.

An hour later he pulled down into an eroded basin, offed saddles and fed an oat issue, watered the mounts scantily on the canteen and pegged them close in on picket pins. He called all his men in on him then and squatted, stick in hand, to draw a sketch in the sand of the action he would fight. For a moment he looked at the half-circle of beard-scrabbled faces and he remembered his reaction to these men the first day he had seen them at the Presidio. The usual lot of regulars, lost men except for a bright-eyed youngster or two: men with no place in the world to go except to the Army, but with roads and towns and schools and churches to follow in the blooded dust of their lone and desperate frontier marches. Twenty-two dog-faced troopers, stenched sour in their filthy shirts, with the sacred sweat of empire, with net a name among them for cutting on any monument. In Cohill himself, as he looked at their faces, there was almost a feeling of devoutness, for he was long gone beyond the trammeling of fear.

He drew a line in the sand. "This is the line of march of the Legion," he said. Then he pointed his stick to the east. "The tribes are strung out in those hills." He made a cross in the sand. "This is our present position. We are between the two forces. The Apaches have seen us and they cannot explain us in any other way—*except that we must be mounted flank guards to the Legion.* What we do to them, the Legion will have done, and they will take their reprisals on it—as well as us. I intend to throw the dog to the dog and to get us out from between the two forces—somehow. There will be no questions. That's all."

When darkness came down, they could see the Legion's bivouac fires strung out for half a mile back at Ogden's Landing, and in the hills to the east, the tiny pinpoints of the Apache fires. At half-past eleven Cohill started his walking approach toward the hills. There were dry washes that they crossed repeatedly, the sands of their winding traces shining white silver in the moonlight. Twice against the moon, as they came in steadily on the low rim of hills, they saw the distant broad-whiskered curtains of rain, smelled water dampening the cooling air.

About an hour after midnight a foot of water came laughing down the broad arroyo they were paralleling. They watered the horses lightly, filled canteens again and moved slowly up the trace of the wash under the shadows of the hills, smelling now and then a faint taint of grease smoke low in the rain-damp air.

They moved in slowly, leading, with the last of the moon throwing its shadows cold behind them. Then across the silence ahead there was a high whinny, and every trooper whipped around fiercely and clamped the nostrils of his own horse against an answer.

Cohill crawled ahead with Corporal Pumphrey, and when they topped the rise, they could see the close-in fires and the Apache ponies watering in the bend of the wash. He sent Pumphrey back to have the horse-holders hold where they were and to bring the men up. When they crawled in on him he bunched them close. For ninety yards along the wash, they had the shore line enfiladed. He opened fire, and the platoon's carbines cut broad like a scythe. Six hundred rounds rapid. There were screams and the ponies thrashed free, galloping up the wash. Bankside fires were kicked out frantically and a few wild shots answered the volleys.

Loaded and locked, the platoon scrambled back on the horse-holders, mounted and pulled out fast the way they had come, heading straight back toward Ogden's Landing and the Legion bivouac.

With an estimated two hours left until dawn, Cohill halted his men about two miles east of the southern end of the bivouac, led down into a draw and holed in to wait. It was so cold now with the late desert night that teeth chattered continuously and the darkness was so thick that one's own hand was lost in it. They sat huddled together for warmth, with the mounts pinned close and the work half done—if it *was* done. And it was; for just before dawn they heard the first dove-call distantly in sleepy love. And another answer it, and another, spreading the sound in a crescent, between them and the hills. Reaching in as the Apache pursuit began to encompass their position.

To the east now, the desert's rim was frosting white. Cohill mounted his platoon, their trouser-facings soaking cold at once with the night damp of the saddle. Then deliberately he walked his tiny command up to flat ground, outlining his men plainly in the fish-belly white light of first dawn. This time there was a bald eagle's scream and suddenly a bunched and ragged gallop of twenty hostiles swinging behind, a mile back across his trail, and off to the east four large groups, fanning out and spacing for individual separate attack.

Toward the Blood River the mist was hazing darker gray, with the breakfast fires of the Legion's strung out bivouac. Cohill's lips drew back. "Satterlee—close up the rear," and he made a hand signal *forward* and jerked it through *trot, gallop—Yo!*

With the light at their backs, but no sun yet, he led his twenty-two men straight down on the Legion at full gallop, whipping them out into platoon front. To his left, two groups of flat riding Coyoteros thundered across to intercept him like a free herd of wild mountain horses. There was an arrogance in the Apache tactic that he had never known before in all his service in the Southwest, an openness of approach to the kill, built on the instinct of victory.

A shot struck the underside of Cohill's left arm as it was up momentarily parallel to the ground, opened it wet and scored the tip of his elbow point in blinding pain. He doubled his fist against it, clenched the forearm and felt the flesh rip wide like a tear in cloth as the muscles contracted. His mount screamed in fury at the spur bite. Behind in the line he saw a trooper pitch off, his mare running free to the right toward the other hostile groups.

The platoon came straight down on the south end of the Legion, with men racing out of the bivouac area to form on their line of flank piquets.

In the narrowing space between, Cohill pulled his platoon sharp right and headed north again, swinging his gallop across the front of the Legion's piquet fire and at right angles to the Apache pursuit. Then the sun burst a hill gap in blinding brass light, and galloping parallel to the bivouac they knew that they were lost to the Legion in the flame and that the Apache attack would come out of it now full upon the bivouac.

Strung out, under sporadic fire from both forces, they galloped between for the getaway, and screaming in their parched throats, seventeen men of his platoon cut back for the Yuma trail with five riderless horses tearing along on their flanks. Fanshaw, Shultz, Pumphrey, Font and Satterlee paid the piper.

Behind them, the first impact on the bivouac was a continuing growl of musketry fire. Then it slacked off. The dust rose over the fight and the heavy firing wound itself down into tattered single shots.

When Cohill got his men well north of Ogden's, he led up a slight rise and halted. Behind them now they could see the fight full joined along the entire line of the bivouac. The clubbed rifles made the ammunition story plain. The Apache cut completely through in three places and regrouped to come back from the river side. They came back to cut through again so that the small resistance perimeters were scattered along the trail with no mutual support possible, like a cattle herd strung out aimlessly against the fanging of a lobo.

With the sun at their backs once more, the Apache concentrated on the south end of the column, isolating it and then overriding it. Then they hauled off to both flanks for flash harassing rushes and hung on to the doomed Legion with their teeth deep sunk in its flesh.

The survivors straggled northward slowly along the trail like a spade-cut snake, with instinct to live, but no ability to sustain its life beyond the stubborn writhe of reflex. Like two cougars that had bowel-torn each other with the instinctive will to kill, the initial intensity of the fight ground itself down to sporadic firing, and by seven o'clock the dust of its final agonies was settling in the burned-off damp of the mists. Badly hurt themselves, the hostiles drew off into the desert in separate groups and the buzzards swung high in the sky. With a veer of the wind, Cohill's men could hear faint screams that had the shocking distant quality of children shrieking at play.

There was no sense of victory in any of their minds, but a feeling of relief and of God-awful weariness of bone. Cohill walked his exhausted command the slow miles north, and two days later they reached Fort Yuma to see the two steamers tied up below the high banks on the western side. Lieutenant Golightly with four of the garrison rowed across to meet him.

Kenneth Golightly was a tall man, bone thin and worn to the raw fiber. He had no word for Cohill, only the will to listen. With eighteen Second Cavalry wounded on his hands and eleven of his own garrison done up bringing them in, he had sixteen men for doubtful duty. Cohill showed him his orders and took command. He had his own men ferried across to the fort and sent Golightly out with a patrol to look for the survivors of the Legion and of Bentinck's expedition.

CHAPTER SIXTEEN

COHILL CAME OUT OF TWENTY-THREE HOURS of board-stiff sleep, with his left arm swollen and hot with fever. He found Sergeant Ohms boiling up coffee in the lean-to. He sent him to locate Lieutenant Golightly, and to get a bottle of carbolic solution. Golightly had fifty-four survivors of the fight in the prison stockade across the river. They had straggled in across the International Line in twos and threes and half squads, Legionnaires and Bentinck's people, throwing down their arms to Golightly's patrol and accepting asylum. Senator Bentinck had been with them.

"There was a Colonel O'Meara with them too," Golightly said. "He died of wounds." Golightly took a notebook and an oilskin packet from his shirt pocket. "He sent his respects to you and asked you to dispose of his effects according to instructions. He requested Catholic burial. We have sent the priest."

Cohill nodded and drank his coffee. He stood for a moment at the window staring out across the tiny sunbaked parade of Fort Yuma. "That's all," he said to Golightly. "Start packing your men to move up-river to relieve Fort Mojave. I will give you the departure time sometime before retreat." He put down his cup. "Swab out this arm of mine, Ohms," and he sat in a chair and braced for the shock of the carbolic.

"Can you read and write, Ohms?"

Ohms shook his head. "Not as good as old Satterlee, sir."

"Do you remember what was said in the cabin of the *Clan Cameron*—the morning I took over under the Sixtieth Article of War?"

"They was going to stop us landing, disarm us or shoot us. Some such."

"That would be about it. I'm going to have it written down for you to sign. I want an affidavit of record."

"Who gets tried, lieutenant?"

"Senator Rutherford Bentinck, for treason."

"Treason, sir?" Ohms' eyes narrowed in their still-swollen sockets and the tip of his tongue snaked his lips. "That's hanging ain't it? By the book?"

"It is," Cohill nodded, "and I want it of record that it is. Here—on the spot while the act of it still reeks. And to high hell with what a reviewing body may do with the verdict later when politics come back into the picture!"

With the nose bandage across his face, Ohms' attempt at a grin was divided into two parts. There was sudden cupidity in his eyes above, and his lips below twisted with his tongue snaking them. "Yes, sir, *lieutenant!*"

Walking out of Golightly's quarters, Cohill stood for a moment breathing deeply of the morning air. Then he crossed to the improvised hospital shed and spoke to the wounded of the Second Cavalry—of the Gila River fight. He walked down the line of pallets, remembering the names where he could, getting the tattered fragments of the massacre story, and with bitterness pressured tight within him, he went then to Second Lieutenant Moseby's quarters that had been given over to him and there faced Rutherford Bentinck. Bentinck was sitting behind Moseby's field desk, writing on a broad piece of foolscap.

He continued writing for a moment, then he looked up with the light of his pale eyes frozen in contained hostility. "I am declaring myself Governor of this Territory." He indicated the paper before him. "And I expect your full support as a federal officer—until I can contact your superiors and have you relieved. That done, I shall have you cashiered."

Cohill reached for the foolscap and wadded it in one hand. "When I invoked the Sixtieth Article of War—" he spoke as if Bentinck were a defaulting corporal whose stripes he would cut "—I placed you in the same category as any one of my troopers. Military personnel. You left the *Clan Cameron* without my order, but I find you now returned to my control. I'm placing you in *close* arrest."

"You're a fool!" Bentinck shouted. "As big a fool as any regular Army officer has ever been when he has set foot beyond the limits of his trade!"

"I am going to try you, senator, for treason, under the Eighty-First Article of War. The penalty is hanging."

Late that night, unable to sleep with the fire that tortured his left arm, he began meticulously to draw up the charges and the specifications and the orders convening Bentinck's court-martial.

For the death penalty that he was determined to have brought in for the record on the spot, it must be a general court-martial with a prescribed minimum of five serving officers as members. Under the Eighth Article of War, he took his authority to convene such a general court as inherent in his written orders from Colonel Alshard, the departmental commander who had delegated court-martial jurisdiction to Cohill under his present status as "the commanding officer of any district or of any force or body of troops, when empowered by the President to do so." Not directly or personally empowered by the President, Cohill construed himself as actually so empowered by the delegation in writing of Alshard's empowerment to him.

Stipulating the Ninth Article of War, Cohill incorporated in his written orders for convening of the court, the fact that "such authority is incident to the power of command, and is independent of the convening officers' own personal rank." Not to disqualify himself as the convening authority, he stipulated Sergeant Ohms as the accuser.

He ordered himself to sit as president of the court with First Lieutenant Golightly, Second Lieutenant Moseby—the agent officer from Ehrenberg, Storekeeper Lieutenant Galloway, and the only surviving officer of the Second Cavalry fight on the Gila, young Second Lieutenant Isham, paralyzed by a shot through his hips, as members. The minimum five for a general court.

Cohill convened the court on the *Cacopah's* upper deck. The members seated themselves on hardtack boxes, Isham prone on his stretcher, as soon as the steamer cast off and started upriver. In the whole history of military justice there is probably no other proceeding of record quite like that one. Five lieutenants sitting on the life of an ex-senator, a one-time brigadier of volunteers. The court came to order under the shadows of Purple Hills Pass, beyond which the river winds due west in its blood-red flow toward Cane Brake Cañon and the Chocolate Mountains.

Bentinck was brought to the upper deck and refused angrily to recognize the authority of the court in any respect. Ignored in his refusal on the grounds that being subject to military law under the Sixtieth Article he had no right to refuse, and warned of his rights to challenge, through cause or peremptorily, he refused even to answer. He made no challenge.

The charge was read to him. Violation of the Eighty-first Article of War, to wit: "Whoever relieves or attempts to relieve the enemy with arms, ammunition, supplies, money or other things, or knowingly harbors or protects or holds correspondence with or gives intelligence to the enemy, either directly or indirectly, shall suffer death or such other punishment as a court martial or military commission may direct."

The specifications traced the steps of Bentinck's defaulting actions, in that he did, by Sergeant Ohms' affidavit, concur in General Barras' revocation of the Treaty of Guadalupe Hidalgo; in that he did, by transcript of the log and manifests of the *Clan Cameron,* certified to by Moxley as master, carry in his expedition supplies, three hundred fifty rounds of modified Whitworth ammunition for the gun battery of the Legion; in that, certified by O'Meara's notebook, actually in his, Bentinck's, own hand, did specify and write out the four terms of capitulation at the mouth of the Colorado; in that, certified by affidavit of the Countess von Hortsendorff, he did, in effect, assume command of the Legion by the fact of giving Colonel O'Meara a direct order to pursue to Howard's by a light flying column the night the steamers passed the narrows. At first Bentinck, asked again for his plea, maintained stubborn silence. Then he shouted, "Not guilty," and the slow flush of anger washed his cheekbones. "You popinjay!" he shouted at Cohill, "you'll be stripped of your shoulder straps and rot in federal prison for this!"

Cohill watched the pale eyes closely. "I'll have you forcibly restrained," he said quietly, "unless you respect this court with your words and actions," and amazingly he saw the shadow of fear dust across Bentinck's eyes. "I'll defend myself," Bentinck snarled, and he stared into the five faces before him. Young men, gone into the weariness of premature age by the hardships of their service. Five junior officers in rank, but gravely and in improvised dignity, the sovereign power of the United States at this time and in this place, with the right to its administration grievously and painfully earned by each one of them, in solemn justice, sitting above the red eroded flow of Blood River—*Lieutenants* River—if you will.

Step by step the case built itself as the *Cacopah* steamed up the great Colorado Valley into the shadows of the Half Way Mountains. In every devious fashion he could, Bentinck made his denials, and in his own angry summation his forensics degenerated into threats and abuse and livid defiance. Cohill had him taken away, and in ten minutes of deliberation the court brought in a verdict of "Guilty of the Charge and Specifications," with the recommendation of death by hanging, just as the steamer passed Bill Williams' Fork and the shadow of Mount Whipple fell broad across her decks.

The next day they steamed slowly along the dramatic line of the Needles and through the slight rapids below Whipple's Crossing.

It was half-past nine at night when Captain Godolphin pulled his whistle cord a mile below the high bluffs of Fort Mojave, on the east bank, and the *Cacopah* breasted up the broadened reach of the Colorado on its final stretch. Lanterns began to wink down the bluff-side paths, and just as they nosed in to tie up, the "C" trumpet above lipped out the nostalgic brass wail of "call to quarters" above the empty miles of the west.

In headquarters, Lieutenant Ames read Cohill's orders and relinquished command. A trace courier was just in that morning overland from the Presidio. Ames handed over two communications addressed to Cohill. The first was from the disbursing officer, the Department of California, the Presidio of San Francisco "…subject officer is herewith notified that overpayment of $122.50 was made in respect to back pay and is due the United States, subject officer not being entitled to horse allowance while detached on Columbia River Survey duties."

The second was a forwarded communication from the agent officer in Portland. "This office is notified that F. Cohill, 1st Lt., 2^{d} Cav. Detached, being first on the regimental promotion list was eligible for promotion to Captain, vice Captain Taylor Danforth resigned. Report being received of Lieutenant Cohill's death on the Columbia River, and his oath not being of record, promotion passes to 1st Lt. Otis Tyne, 2^{d} Cav."

Cohill stood up wearily. "I have a prisoner under sentence of death aboard the *Cacopah*, Ames. I want him guardhoused while his trial papers are sent to San Francisco." Ames whistled softly when Cohill told him the rest of it. He said, "You'll never hang him." Cohill nodded. "I knew that when I brought him to trial. I merely wanted his conviction on record. What will probably happen is that he'll go scot-free to hang me—and the department commander. Everyone else has tried to."

Down at the wharfside, the relief garrison was filing off with its personal equipment. Above them, Sergeant Ohms was standing by the wheel cubby. It seemed to Cohill that he could see the man's eyes long before he saw the outline of his body, and it seemed to him also that in some peculiar way he knew what Ohms was going to say to him long before he framed the question. There is a strange affinity at times between diverse people, wherein men may meet each other from opposite ends of the earth and find their missing facets of character written plain in each other.

"Where's the prisoner, Ohms?"

Sergeant Ohms straightened up, brought his heels together. "The lieutenant ain't *heard,* sir?"

"Heard what?"

Ohms' hands moved slightly at his sides, as if he would look at them for stain, then remembering that he had washed them. "Senator Bentinck must've hanged himself, sir. The guard found him that way not ten minutes gone. What would you call that— retribution mebbe?"

"What would you call it, Ohms?"

"Well I don't know, lieutenant." Ohms' lips twisted in that grimace of his. "I sure wouldn't call it no *direct* order, sir. Down at Yuma I mean—when you said treason."

"Ohms," Cohill looked at him. "*Some day!*"

"Yes, sir."

Fifteen minutes later, when Cohill and 'Theena had climbed the bluff to her allocated quarters and he had left her to bathe and dress, Lieutenant Ames tapped at Cohill's door while he was bathing. "There was a third letter from the Presidio for you. From Colonel Alshard, marked personal, so here it is." "Dear Cohill. Under anonymous accusation that you had accepted bribe of $50,000, I investigated the matter at Wells Fargo's bank and have affidavit from them that deposit was made by one Ramillies Moktir, servant to Bentinck, and that you were not a physical party to the transaction. I suggest that if Bentinck makes accusation against you on this count that you at once ask for a board on the matter."

Before Cohill could get into the second paragraph there was another knock on his door. Sergeant Ohms. "Yes, Ohms?" Ohms hesitated slightly, looked off into the shadows. He said, "Being as old Satterlee's dead, I'm senior. Sort of acting top soldier, you might say. So took m'own permission to speak to the lieutenant."

"Speak up."

"About the half-cut on the money, sir. That's out. I won't take a cent. You earned it all."

For a moment it was pure Greek to Cohill. He stared into Ohms' shifting eyes. "I just don't like officers, sir," the man said. "That's why I bought in that night when I heard Houget put it to you about the fifty thousand. But I got to like you—a whole lot—sir. So you keep all of it —you and the lady."

For the first time in two years Cohill snorted in spontaneous laughter. "Ohms," he said, "you'll have to take it. Your share anyway." And he showed him the draft and the colonel's letter. "For I shall send the whole thing to the disabled soldiers' fund, and you'll need help from it some day—if somebody doesn't get you first."

"Yes, *sir*," Ohms said solemnly. "I guess so, sir—but not so long's I go by the book. Treason gets hanging—as well as murder."

When he had gone, Cohill read the second paragraph of Colonel Alshard's letter. "If you have reached Fort Mojave by the time this gets to you, it will be some reward to you that the reply from Second Cavalry Headquarters, Tucson (through Leavenworth as usual), to my wire informing them of your temporary duty states that you are eligible to promotion to captain vice Captain Otis Tyne, deceased, and to major, vice Captains Blenkinship, Schuyler and Juneau, also deceased. Cordially, McC. Alshard."

With taps beginning to sound on the C trumpet from head-quarters, Cohill opened his door and stood for a moment until the call ran itself out. He looked across under the close broad canopy of desert stars toward the quarters that had been given 'Theena and he was conscious of a completeness that lies beyond all words. It was on him in firm conviction that nothing at all important had ever happened to either of them before, and that anything that was ever to have real significance was starting its slow march down the years to meet them.

Then, because he was what he was and would always be, in spite of everything else, words began to form in his mind. "I'll clean up the final details to-morrow—write my report—and get out east to Tucson. To rejoin my regiment."

Printed in Great Britain
by Amazon